A SURGEON'S TALE

WILLIAM LYNES

Black Rose Writing | Texas

ISBN: 978-1-68513-495-2
LIBRARY OF CONGRESS CONTROL NUMBER: 2024936990
PUBLISHED BY BLACK ROSE WRITING
www.blackrosewriting.com

Printed in the United States of America
Suggested Retail Price (SRP) $19.95

A Surgeon's Tale is printed in Garamond Premier Pro

*As a planet-friendly publisher, Black Rose Writing does its best to eliminate unnecessary waste to reduce paper usage and energy costs, while never compromising the reading experience. As a result, the final word count vs. page count may not meet common expectations.

I would like to dedicate this book to my Lord and Savior, Jesus Christ.
–William Lynes

PRAISE FOR
A SURGEON'S TALE

"In William Lynes's gripping sequel to *A Surgeon's Knot*, *A Surgeon's Tale*, readers are again immersed in the intense world of surgical training at the fictional University Medical Center in Northern California.

For fans of Lynes's previous works and enthusiasts of medical thrillers alike, *A Surgeon's Tale* is a must-read. It not only captivates readers with its thrilling narrative but also offers a poignant exploration of the human experience in the demanding world of medicine."
–Website: http://GinaRaeMitchell.com

"*A Surgeon's Tale* is a brilliant work of fiction and shows the intersection of conflicted healthcare professionals with desperate people who are critically ill, mentally ill, or are dangerous to society. Told by a compassionate physician, the reader will deeply care about the characters who are not always as they initially appear and who have nearly impossible circumstances to surmount."
–Rebecca Farnbach, Author of Dancing With Prayers in My Feet

"*A Surgeon's Tale*" by William Lynes, a riveting sequel to the captivating novel "*A Surgeon's Knot,*" grips readers from beginning to end. In this tale, every cut tells a story, and every suture holds determination. Prepare to be enchanted by the cut-throat world of surgery from the first page to the final stitch."
–Cyra A. Blogger & Owner @ The Literary Vault

"I just finished another fine read by William. Lynes, MD as he pulls you into his world.

His uncanny talent of spot-on word descriptions of people is akin to a blue-ribbon chef concocting another fine meal. You'll find *A Surgeon's Tale* to be an irresistible book from cover to cover. Enjoy your meal."
–WD Stauffer, retired printer

"A Surgeon's Tale is a terrific follow-up to *A Surgeon's Knot*. I really enjoyed reading about the growth of the characters. Jackson Cooper, M.D., is making his way through the next stage of his residency and his life. It is a great insight into what a new surgeon has to deal with and what they see and experience. Real behind-the-scenes goings-on that are just so interesting and so few people are privy to. William Lynes really grasps the essence of this time in a young surgeon's life; I was enthralled and couldn't put it down."
–Timothy P Loughran, Mortgage Loan Professional

"Step into the world of 'A Surgeon's Tale,' where the lives of Dr. Jackson Cooper and Dr. Patrice Summers intertwine in a narrative crafted with profound empathy and compassion. Written from the heart of someone intimately familiar with the challenges of the medical profession, this book delves into the complexities of human connection, resilience, and the pursuit of healing. Drawing from William Lynes' own experiences as a physician, surgeon, and patient, the characters of Jackson and Patrice come to life with authenticity and depth. Through their trials and triumphs, readers are invited to explore the profound impact of empathy and understanding in the realm of healthcare. 'A Surgeon's Tale' is not just a story—it's a testament to the power of compassion to transform lives, both on and off the operating table."
–Daniel Dow, MD

ACKNOWLEDGEMENTS

I would like to acknowledge the artwork on the back cover, a beautiful image of a scalpel containing surgeon's gloved hand by Dr. Tom Paluch: Surgeon, Savage Artist, and Humble Sculptor of Human Flesh. San Diego, California.

A

SURGEON'S

TALE

CHAPTER 1

The bald-headed man sat on the rumbling gray motorcycle. Tension filled his eyes, one brown, one green, their colors highlighted in the disappearing sun. He wore a tattered gray German army uniform with a silver *Doppellitze,* double braid insignia accenting his collar. His eyes searched the rolling field covered with moist green grass, fright apparent on his strained face. He strapped the Nazi helmet on his head, the enemy always present. Checking the gas tank between his legs for petrol, he revved the BMW engine and raced off, dirt flying from a spinning rear tire.

The man raced through the occupied hamlet, blasting over the dirty cobblestone streets. Ahead was a manned checkpoint with its gate down, and he exploded through the wooden postern, scattering the Nazi jack-booted soldiers. A high-speed chase began, with shots ringing out and side-car motorcycles pursuing the fleeing man through winding roads and across open fields.

Before him stood a low razor wire fence, obstructing his escape to the cloud-covered horizon. He skidded to a stop, then turned to see the following stalkers. Far ahead lay freedom, arrival blocked by a soft grass-covered berm flanking the obstructing fence.

Shots struck the ground, ricocheting dirt up around the man. He could hear the roaring motorbikes approaching and knew they would soon be upon him. He debated, his escape versus capture tormenting him.

With a blast of the motorbike, exhaust billowed from the pipes, tires spun, and the bike twisted ahead in a spray of dirt. The cycle climbed the berm, and the man stopped and accessed the barricaded fence. Breathing heavily now, he unlatched and tossed his helmet toward the gathering mob. Turning around, he raced his motorcycle down to the foot of the knoll. With his pursuers gathering around him, he blasted away up the berm, taking flight, and clearing the fence in a beautiful crest at the vertex.

He crashed down on the rear tire; the bike zigzagging as the rider attempted to control the mechanical beast. Shots rang out from the military group, stopping their pursuit at the fence. The man lifted his front tire from the dirt road in victory and sped away to safety.

●   ●   ●   ●   ●

The white-coated physicians and nurses stood around the foot of the hospital bed like a menagerie of pale birds of prey. It was morning rounds, with the collection gathering to manage patients.

Interested now in the patient, the assembly focused on the intern. He was a man with tossed straw-colored hair and three-day facial growth. Michael Nelson, MD, wore a green surgical scrub suit, a wrinkled white coat, and red loafer-type tennis shoes. He looked at a note card and presented the patient to the group.

"Maurice, or Maury Latinsky, is a 37-year-old white male with GRID."

"Let's use the term AIDS, or at least HIV, Michael." The chief resident, Tara Patel, spoke up, correcting the intern. She, a tall woman, wore the day's uniform - a white coat and scrubs. Black piercing eyes and a short-cut black head of hair stylized the leader of the group. GRID, or Gay Related Immune Disease, was the first term given to the HIV/AIDS disease in the early 1980s. It was 1983, and the modern term HIV/AIDS was being used.

Mike agreed with the terminology and continued. "He's now a week after a right nephrectomy and drainage of a tuberculous renal and perinephric abscess." The patient had a kidney tuberculosis abscess related to his AIDS condition, treated with surgical removal of the kidney.

Maurice lay in his bed, soaked white sheets scattered around his feet. He began thrashing about amid a fever-induced rigor. Tara asked: "does he have a fever, Michael?"

The intern snapped up the bedside clipboard hanging on the foot of the bed. "His temp's now 103? That was after I saw him this morning, just fifteen minutes ago. Then his temp was normal." Mike took his presentation seriously, upset that he missed the man's fever. He looked at Tara, somewhat embarrassed.

Tara tried to comfort the intern. "These AIDS fevers spike like that, Michael," referring to the tendency of AIDS patients to have sudden fevers.

Mike appreciated the information and seemed relieved. As an intern, his job was to know everything about the urology service before anyone else. He was a hardworking fellow who graduated from the USC School of Medicine, now a surgery intern at the University Medical Center, or UMC

"Look at the sweat on his forehead, that shaking. It's a rigor, a shaking chill from fever. Some Tylenol. He needs some Tylenol!" Tara stepped to the bedside. She wiped the man's bald head with a tissue.

Maurice was awake, snarling a loud growl. He opened his left eye, revealing a suspicious green eyeball glaring at the woman. The group recoiled in fear as the man leaped onto the bed rail, barking like a hound. "Krauts... goons. They're everywhere, Freddie!"

The intern grabbed the man's waving arm. He moved to his side and led him to sit back on the bed. "Freddie's not here, Mr. Latinsky." He turned to the group and said, "Freddie's his partner."

Sarah was a neatly dressed, attractive nurse. She stepped forward with a disturbing piece of information. "He's been drinking his urine, Dr. Patel. I took away his urinal this morning. I think he is really thirsty!"

"You're kidding, Sarah? He has been NPO for a week now." Realizing the truth before the nurse could answer, NPO being nothing per oral, Tara went on. She asked the group: "can we feed him? Are you thirsty, Mr. Latinsky?" She moved to the patient and examined his abdomen and right flank incision. Using her stethoscope, she listened to the man's belly. "He has good bowel sounds. Michael, let's start him on full liquids." Mike made a quick note on his clipboard.

Maurice seemed more awake; his rigor now passed. He smiled a sly smile and lay back in his bed. "I thought the goons were after me, Dr. Tara."

"Goons? Whatever do you mean, Mr. Latinsky?"

"You know, Goons ... krauts. They were after me. I got away." The man smiled, his mouth full of red, swollen gums. He appeared quite wasted; He seemed, however, proud of an imaginary escape from the German army.

The group went into the hallway, stopping to finish with Mr. Latinsky.

"You should note his heterochromatic eyes, students. His irises are green and brown; the different colors are called heterochromatic." Tara washed her hands, drying them on a paper towel as she walked to the group's center.

Jackson Cooper was the junior resident on the urology service. "Tara, the fact that Latinsky had TB in the right kidney, doesn't that imply that he has TB throughout his urinary tract?"

"You know I have been researching that subject, Jackson. Stay tuned to grand rounds on Saturday. It is on urologic tuberculosis. Anyway, TB gets into the urinary tract through blood seeding. If it is in the right kidney, yes, it is in the left. Our only option is anti-tuberculosis drugs. We need infectious disease to see him." She turned to the intern. "Michael, call ID. Describe his case. I think he should be on triple TB drugs, but see what they say." With that, they moved on.

•   •   •   •   •

The man marched down the hallway, dressed in a tailored beige velour coat and an oversized green hand-tied silk bowtie. Pressed black slacks, their cuffs touching the shiny ox-blood polished penny loafer shoes with vintage coinage, completed his ensemble. He was carrying a bundle of red and pink flowers; roses, carnations, and chrysanthemums. As he passed the group of physicians, he nodded to the assembly and continued into Maurice Latinsky's room.

"Why is it so dark in here, dear?" The man moved to the window, drew the curtain aside, and awakened the room. He tossed the old wilted flowers into the trash and placed the new bundle in the glass vase. He moved to the patient and embraced the man. "Maury, why your sheets are completely soaked."

Maury sat on the bedside, his stick-like legs hanging out under his gown. "Freddie, I am so glad you're here. I had that dream again."

"The Great Escape? Are you Steve McQueen, dear?"

"Captain Virgil Hilts, the Cooler King." Maury looked down and sighed. He coughed up a wad of blood-tinged sputum and deposited it into the yellow emesis basin with a spit. As he looked at Freddie, he appeared on the verge of tears. "It was so real, Freddie! The goons. They almost had me this time!"

"Did you jump the fence?"

Maury coughed a rumbling cough. He stood gingerly and hugged his friend. "Yes, I was almost flying. I cleared the fence by a mile. Almost lost it on the landing, though. But I was flying at the end. Wish I could fly out of this place."

"You're so awake today, dear. You look marvelous. Yesterday you were mumbling to yourself so much. You were in your shell and didn't seem to know that I was here. I brought you this Polaroid of your baby, Maury. Suzette just had her hair styled. She misses her daddy!" Freddie gave the man a small picture.

Maury took the photo. He seemed unsure of who it was, a cute curly black-haired miniature poodle. A smile came over his face as the man realized the dog's identity. He lay back down in bed, clutching the photograph to his chest. He gazed upward for a while. With a struggle, he turned onto his side and faced Freddie. "My mind, it's going, Freddie! It comes and goes. Sometimes I have no idea where I am."

"It's okay, dear. You'll be going home very soon."

CHAPTER 2

The hospital call was hectic. There was little sleep to be had. A new day dawned, and Jackson Cooper expected another long, busy one. At task were consultations from the hospital requesting an urologic evaluation. The weight of responsibility rested heavily on his shoulders as a junior resident on the UMC urology service.

He stood that morning in the urology resident's office. It was a cramped room filled with old wooden desks, a well-used pot of burnt-tasting coffee, and a wall of incoming department mail niches. The department secretary recorded phone calls for consultations in a small, tattered ring binder in the mailbox. Today three new consults filled the book, an entire morning of labor for the overworked urology resident.

With messy brown hair, Jackson stood just under six feet tall, in need of a haircut. He had friendly, smoky blue eyes covered with heavy brown, rimmed aviator-shaped glasses. The resident wore an alternative uniform comprising a white button-down shirt, a hastily tied blue and white striped tie, brown corduroy cuffed pants, and a wrinkled white coat. He stood with style, however, in his signature scuffed carrot-colored iguana cowboy boots.

He sighed, considering the impending work. He scanned the binder of consults. There was a 75-year-old male with a history of prostate cancer. Completing the consults were a pediatric cancer patient with nighttime wetting or enuresis, and a 45-year-old female with a persistent urinary tract infection (UTI) and fever. The clinic begins soon, so he must see all patients promptly. He worked from the end of the list, tackling first the UTI in a woman named Gloria Sands on the internal medicine service.

Jackson looked over his shoulder, confirming that he was alone. A brown leather attaché case with a candy red stripe sat on the floor by the corner desk. He lifted the case, a Christmas gift from his sister, and opened the briefcase with a pop. Retrieving a large prescription bottle, he opened the vial, shook out, and downed two oval white tablets. Herein lay the ritual. He turned the bottle in his hand and read the pharmacy label. Dated one year before, in the summer of 1982, the pharmacy label marked the bottle as containing the opioid Percocet. He headed to the consults and the ward.

Gloria Sands was an overweight woman with a pageboy cut of blonde hair. She had close-set hazel eyes, which seemed too small for her plump face. The woman covered them with green and black leopard pattern cat-shaped glasses secured with a pearl-beaded eyeglass chain. When Jackson entered the room, she was very distracted, laughing and applauding the wall-mounted television broadcast of Jeopardy.

"Ms. Sands. I am Dr. Cooper from the urology department. Your doctor, Dr. Fitzgerald, asked me to review your case." Jackson reached over and shook the preoccupied woman's hand, pulled up a chair, and sat at the bedside. "Now I understand you have been having fevers for a couple of weeks, right?" The patient seemed distracted, constantly glancing at the broadcast without listening. Jackson reached for the off switch on the set. "Can I shut this off?"

Gloria glanced at the resident, checking his nametag and then his face. Grudgingly she said: "yeah ... yes... sure ... I don't care. What was your name?"

"Dr. Cooper. From urology. I understand you have been having fevers for a couple of weeks."

Gloria slipped her glasses off, letting them hang on her chest. "Yes... my Mr. Whiskers... I found Mr. Whiskers on the kitchen floor. Fevers. I've had a fever ever since then."

"Mr. Whiskers? Who's Mr. Whiskers?"

"My cat, Mr. Whiskers, is my cat."

"Your cat? Was your cat dead?"

"Absent ... I prefer the term absent, Jackson."

For now, Jackson allowed the use of his first name. At least she didn't call him Jack, his dreaded nickname. "I'm confused. What did the cat have to do with the fever? Do you know Ms. Sands?"

"I don't know. Shouldn't you tell me that?"

"So, you've been having fevers every day since then... since your cat became absent?"

Despite being distracted, Gloria nodded a bored yes. "You know fevers; I get them all the time, Jackson."

"Cooper... it's Dr. Cooper." The interview continued. Burning during urination was a recurring issue for her. She indicated a history of many urinary infections, always related to her cat's health. Jackson completed patient queries, excused himself, and headed to the nursing station.

Jackson searched for the patient's old hospital chart, showing any prior medical visits or hospitalizations. Filed in an old gray file cabinet in the S's was an empty chart folder labeled with the patient's name. Ms. Sands never visited UMC before. He looked at the ongoing in-patient hospital chart. Her urine had an E. coli bacterium in it. The bacteria responded to the IV antibiotics taken by the patient for a week. He looked at her vital sign record. A daily temperature fever spike of 102 to 103 degrees Fahrenheit occurred for the last two weeks.

If Ms. Sands had a urinary tract infection, any associated fever would typically resolve with adequate antibiotics in less than three days. Given her urine culture and IV antibiotics, she should have been without a fever. Complicated UTIs with either a kidney abscess or obstruction of the ureter, the tube connecting the kidney and bladder, could explain the persistence of fever. He would check her x-rays and present the patient to his attending physician.

•　　•　　•　　•　　•

They met each early a.m. five days a week in the classroom at the university. The room had rows of metal folding chairs, an old wooden podium, and a huge urn of brewing bitter-tasting coffee. Lee W. Hickok, MD, poured himself some in a Styrofoam cup on which was carved LWH and walked to the front of the room. "Hello, I'm Lee W., and I am an alcoholic."

Lee W. was a man in his forties, with dark brown hair highlighted on the temples with gray and wearing round glasses. He dressed in a brown plaid sports coat with a pair of distinctive cowboy boots, shiny black and snakeskin in construction. He introduced the meeting, speaking with a suggestion of a South Texan accent.

"We have business this morning. Teddy is going to make the report."

A large nurse dressed in a white tunic stood and approached the podium. "Hello, group. I am Teddy, and I am an alcoholic and a drug addict."

"Hello, Teddy," the audience recited in unison.

The man began a presentation of local fund-raising activities for that month. He reported as a treasurer, mentioning monies coming in and going out. Karen was next, a neatly dressed woman of around fifty in a conservative skirt and high-heel shoes. "God grant me the serenity to accept the things I cannot change, courage to change the things I can, and wisdom to know the difference." An Alcoholic Anonymous meeting then proceeded. Initially, they read the twelve steps. A short testimony about a life of alcoholism from a tall black cafeteria employee followed.

After a brief break, Lee W. Hickok returned to the podium. "Well, ya'll, you have the unfortunate distinction of having me give the long testimonial. I am Lee W., and I am an alcoholic."

"Hello, Lee W."

"I stole my stepfather's whiskey and drank under the porch when I was twelve." Lee W. took a handwritten notepaper out of his pocket, balled it up, and threw his prepared talk across the room for effect.

"He beat me quite a bit for anything else he could think of. Honestly, drinking was the only thing that brute gave me. Soon, I couldn't live without it. I drank daily and frequently, heck I drank all the time, really, since that day. My mother died in front of me. She had taken me away from him in the dead of night. They were fighting again; he was a rough one. He broadsided us at the intersection. I still see her dead eyes and blood-soaked face in my dreams."

Lee W. described a life of alcoholism, carousing, and drugs. At one point, he withdrew himself from the alcohol, treating the resulting DTs or delirium tremens with an IV and valium. His sobriety did not last.

"I was sober for just one year after that. Drinking again became my tool. I am a surgeon, and not proud to say I was drunk during my medical practice and even surgeries. I dabbled with cocaine and tried to kill myself after my wife Amber left me last summer." Lee W. held up his healed forearm laceration for all to see.

"I am sober now for fourteen months. It has been 421 days now. Without God, I wouldn't be here. I live one day at a time."

●　　　●　　　●　　　●　　　●

He was just leaving the meeting when his pager went off. "This is Dr. Hickok. Someone paged me."

"Lee W., it's Jackson. Are you the unlucky attending on call today?"

"Hell, yeah. Y'all got something for me?" His life was exhilarating after becoming sober. Lee W. now lived for medicine and surgery. He smiled at the phone, anxious about medical problems to solve.

"Just three consults. I need to present them to you, though."

"Can y'all meet me in my office?"

Lee W. Hickok was a newly appointed associate professor of urology at the UMC in Northern California. The university was a teaching institution, well respected as a leader in modern American medicine. His office, however, did little to reinforce the importance of his professorship. It was a cramped, eight-by-ten-foot room, with the door opening into the department's tiny kitchen. A MacIntosh computer and a sizeable dot-matrix printer filled an old oak desk that dominated the small room.

Jackson arrived as the attending urologist was just opening the office door. "Grab us a couple of coffees, my fellow teetotaler. And remember fondly adding just a drop of the good stuff for me."

Jackson turned and moved to the coffee urn in the resident's office. He wasn't sure about the Texan's last remark. Yes, Jackson was a recovering narcotic addict. Lee W. was supposedly a sober alcoholic. Last year, during Jackson's surgery internship, he drank with Lee W. in that same office. On multiple occasions, he added a few shots to the man's coffee. Guess he is just reminiscing, he thought. Before he left with the coffee, Jackson quickly opened his attaché case. He grabbed the prescription bottle and shoved it into his white coat pocket.

Lee W. sat back in his office chair, his booted feet on the edge of his cramped desk. A smiley logo screensaver circled harmlessly on the computer screen. Jackson handed the porcelain cup to the man. He pulled over a cardboard box of books, sat, and drank his coffee.

"Did you freshen this up for me?" Lee W. sipped the hot brew loudly, a sly smile on his face.

"Yeah, Lee W., sweet amber, just like you like." Jackson put his cup on the edge of the desk. He reached into his pocket and pulled out the prescription bottle. He shook out two oval white tablets and threw them into his mouth. "You want a couple?"

As Lee W. placed his feet on the ground, a look of curiosity and shock crossed his face.

"Here, they're just Tic Tacs!" Jackson shook a couple of breath mints into the Texan's hand. "I keep this bottle. It helps." He read the prescription on the bottle. "Percocet—dispense one hundred. One or two tabs orally every three to four hours as needed for pain. It's dated June 23, 1982."

"One year ago, I see. Jackson, these are the most delicious Tic Tacs. You're a strong man, my friend."

They decided the disposition of the first two of the consult patients in Lee W.'s office. Mr. James Simpson was a 75-year-old black male with widespread metastatic prostate cancer on the internal medicine service. He was suffering from horrible pain because of the boney spread of his cancer. Dr. Charles Huggins won the 1966 Nobel Prize. The revolutionary finding put most patients in temporary remission after removing testicles and testosterone. Jackson would arrange an OR time this week to perform a bilateral orchiectomy, a surgical removal of the man's testicles.

Kenny Tobias was a six-year-old boy with leukemia. He was on the oncology service and was receiving chemotherapy. He had a problem with nighttime bedwetting or enuresis.

"Should we start him on Tofranil, Lee W.?" Tofranil is an oral medication that relaxes the bladder. Taken at bedtime, it was commonly effective in enuresis.

Lee W. reached for a xeroxed medical article. "Here's what we're going to do for that child, y'all." He tossed an article into Jackson's lap. The piece's title, *Treatment of Persistent Enuresis with Desmopressin Nasal Spray*, was highlighted in yellow. "It's new, Y'all. It's also called DDAVP or desmopressin. The nasal spray cuts down the kidney's urine production at night. It has much fewer side-effects than Tofranil."

Lee W. wanted to see the UTI patient with persistent fever, Gloria Sands. Her problem was that she continued to spike daily fevers after seven days of intravenous antibiotics.

"She relates this fever to the death of her cat, Lee W. The cat's name was Mr. Whiskers. She found him dead on the kitchen floor, and she has had a fever ever since. There is something peculiar about her, however. Sort of distracted. Almost unconcerned about the problem. Just a touch odd, I think."

At the patient's door, Jackson handed the vital sign sheet to Lee W. "See," Jackson said, pointing to the graphic tracing of her temperature. "She spikes a 102 to 103 fever each day at three p.m.. You know, Lee W., look at this. That's just after shift change!"

Lee W. looked at his watch. "That's in thirty minutes, Jackson. Let's go see her."

A closed bedside curtain faced them when the two entered the patient's room. The television was blasting a daytime soap of some sort.

The room was dark; all lights were turned off. Jackson dragged back the curtain. "Ms. Sands, it's Dr. Cooper."

"Stay out. You troll!" the patient yelled.

The patient sat with head raised on the bed. She was busy fumbling with her left arm and IV sight. Jackson grabbed her arm. She was injecting the syringe into the IV line. He removed the syringe and stood looking at the woman, incredulously.

"That's mine, Jack!" The roused patient stood quickly at the bedside and wrestled Jackson for the syringe.

Jackson grabbed both arms of the thrashing woman. Lee W. stepped beyond the woman and reached into an open bedside drawer. Within was a specimen cup of clear fluid. In the bottom was debris, brown and green leafy material.

The woman started crying. "That's my stuff. Now leave! Rape! Rape!" The woman stomped her feet, jumping back into the bed. She pulled the sheet over her face. "Leave me alone, you perverts."

Two nurses hurried into the room. "Dr. Cooper, what's happening?"

Jackson and Lee W. left the crying woman with the nurses. They moved to the hallway and eventually sat in the nursing station.

"That's stool," Lee W. said. He held the container up to the light, shaking it gently, the debris in the bottom now dispersed through the liquid.

Jackson took the container from Lee W. He compared the syringe to the fluid in the specimen jar. The two looked identical. "What the heck?"

"She injects her stool into her IV. There is your source of fever, Jackson."

"Munchausen, she's a Munchausen, Lee W.!"

Baron von Munchausen was an 18th-century German officer known for embellishing his life and experience stories. Munchausen syndrome is a severe factitious disorder where someone pretends to be ill repeatedly. Considered a mental illness, Munchausen syndrome is associated with severe emotional difficulties.

Gloria Sands left the hospital quickly. She refused to sign her against medical advice (AMA) forms. Knowing the course of Munchausen syndrome patients, her appearance in other medical institutions with identical claims was likely.

CHAPTER 3

Jackson Cooper took a deep breath as he hesitantly knocked on the heavy wooden door. He was tentative, anticipating a harsh confrontation from the crotchety inhabitant who reminded him of a character in a nineteenth century Dicken's novel.

"Come in," the voice crackled.

Within the ancient office sat Elmer J. Crabb, MD, professor emeritus, sipping tea noisily from a white china cup and sitting in a straight-back leather armchair. The man was frail, with thin white hair that scattered easily. Despite his age, his face displayed a youthful pinkness and only occasional wrinkles. Dressed in a double-breasted, brass-buttoned, navy-blue blazer, he wore a button-down collared white shirt. Dr. Crabb's ensemble continued with neatly pressed black pleated slacks and a hand-tied crimson bowtie. He wore little, shiny polished, ox-blood leather wingtip brogues. Jackson knew from prior contacts that they clicked as he walked.

The dim room's air smelled strangely ancient, stale, and cold. To the doctor's right sat a small round-topped wooden table adorned with an antique brass lamp that flickered as if old. On the table was a rye bread sandwich, missing just a single bite. Jackson had heard from departmental tales that it contained canned salty sardines and a kosher dill pickle, and he often confirmed this with his breath. A pink frosted cupcake with a single candle sat beside the partially eaten meal.

"Dr. Cooper, to what do I owe your illustrious appearance today?"

"Grand rounds are beginning, Dr. Crabb. Tara asked me to remind you."

"Dr. Patel surely knows I am aware of the meeting, Dr. Cooper. I may be 104 years old today, but I will never avoid my responsibilities. Reckless, young, and foolish. To put it mildly, this generation is imprudent. Couldn't find your neck, a tie, or your face with a razor this morning, Dr. Cooper?"

Jackson looked down at his attire. He dressed quickly this morning in a wrinkled white coat and a second day of the same green scrub suit. Wearing an unshaven stubble, and except for his polished cowboy boots, the urology resident stood embarrassed by his appearance. He looked up self-consciously and tried to divert the professor's daunting gaze. "That cupcake, it must be for your birthday. Congratulations, Dr. Crabb."

"Big whoop!" The professor said with a pan-face. The intimidating man slowly set the teacup on the table. With some difficulty, he stood, smoothed the front of his blazer, and straightened his bowtie. With a steady grasp, he picked up the cupcake. Shuffling slowly past Jackson, he pulled out the candle and tossed it in the trash. He then handed the pastry to the resident with an admonition. "You better eat this, Dr. Cooper. If you do not, you will not please my lovely wife, Eleanor."

As EJC, the professor emeritus, disappeared down the hallway like a keen cricket, everyone could hear clicking brogues. The resident glanced at him, feeling relieved. To spite him, Tara purposely gave out this assignment to retrieve the professor that morning. Quite a formidable task for Jackson. She knew his disposition well, likely chuckling to herself. Everyone at the university avoided the man. Jackson's partial survival pleased him that day as he followed the professor. Relieved, the resident glanced at the man and headed to the meeting.

•   •   •   •   •

Grand rounds were a didactic meeting of the University Medical Center's urologic physicians and nurses. Every Saturday, the Kenneth George

Bolton Auditorium holds an event. It is at the end of the hall, close to the urologic offices. Over the door was a flashy stainless steel lettered sign highlighted by small Christmas tree bulbs announcing the place's name. The room and chairman were called KGB, referencing Russian intelligence.

Two imposing portraits dominated the front of the auditorium, each lit by an overhead spotlight. One painting was KGB, the chairman, and the other EJC, the professor emeritus. Both stared at the crowd with intimidating pouts and neatly tied bow ties. Steel folding chairs filled the room, with a large projector screen covering the front wall.

The KGB Hall began filling with local urologists and other medical personnel. The room's capacity was 200, and as the group filed in, no seat appeared empty. Kenneth George Bolton entered from the front side door and sat in his reserved wooden rocking chair in the front row. He signaled to Mike Nelson, the sandy-haired intern, who retrieved his always-present cup of C, or hot chocolate, for him. KGB was a middle-aged round man with a balding tonsured head of white hair and blue piercing eyes covered with rimless spectacles. Like the professor emeritus, he always wore hand-tied bow ties in distinct patterns and colors. He had dressed today in his favorite seersucker suit. He spoke with a good old boy North Carolinian accent, which he always embellished.

Tara Patel stood nervously with a microphone in front of the crowded room. It was Saturday, and her responsibility to present something worthy in grand rounds was beginning. "Let's get going, people. Please get to your seats." She waited for the minglers to sit down and then started. "Today, we are discussing an interesting case of urinary tuberculosis." Tara then began telling the group about a patient now in the hospital on her urology service.

"M.L. is a 38-year-old white male with HIV/AIDS and renal tuberculosis. A week ago, Dr. Bolton and our staff performed a simple nephrectomy and drained a perinephric tuberculous abscess." The chairman had nothing to contribute.

Tara told about the patient, his presentation with fever and pain, his immunocompromised status secondary to HIV/AIDS, his evaluation, and his surgery. She continued discussing the literature concerning TB and its infections in the urinary tract.

TB was already an unusual disease in 1983 because of antibiotics. First developed in the World War II era with sulfa drugs and penicillins, antibiotics quickly revolutionized the treatment of infections, including those secondary to TB. Few modern medicine physicians were familiar with treating patients without antibiotics. In the audience was one of those physicians, Doctor Elmer J. Crabb, whose anger was brewing, his face getting pinker.

"Doctor Bolton, do you have anything you want to add?" Tara finished her presentation, and as per protocol, she opened the floor to questions and comments. First, however, was an opportunity for the urology chairman to pontificate.

KGB handed his Styrofoam cup of C to the intern. He stood with some deliberation as Tara rushed the handheld microphone to his side. "Well, y'all, that was a super, just a super presentation, Tara. We don't much more see TB anymore. Scarce as hen's teeth, it is. Maury, the patient, and his GRID are set up for TB. Tara. You were so right on with your prompt surgical exploration. I am sure y'all have him on the road to recovery."

It was clear the chairman had little to contribute. He looked around the nearly full room, picking out one of his colleagues. "Lee W., what experiences with these pesky infections can you shine a light on for us?"

Lee W. Hickok was sitting in the audience, dozing off, perhaps dreaming of a stiff drink of sweet amber. The urologist was also a man of the south, remembered all too often his undignified exit from Galveston, Texas. Dressed today in iguana-skin cowboy boots, he slowly stood and cleared his throat. "Well, y'all, you see these cases on the border occasionally in illegals with TB all over their bodies. Ah... y'all. Know what? We have a distinguished surgeon here with us. Dr. Crabb practiced during a time when such cases were extremely common. Perhaps Dr. Crabb could clue us in on this interesting case."

Elmer J. Crabb was sitting in the back with a scowl. Evidently, he was not happy with the presentation, which was his nature. With great difficulty, he struggled to his feet and spoke. With some concern, Tara hurried down the center aisle, dragging the microphone and cord. "Here, Dr. Crabb, use this."

"Do I need such a blasted thing?" he said, rejecting the mic. He threw it at a spectator on his right. "I have just one question for you, Dr. Bolton. Did you perform a simple nephrectomy or a nephroureterectomy on this queer?"

Some were now chuckling in the audience. EJC questioned whether the surgery removed only the kidney, a simple nephrectomy, or both the kidney and the ureter, a nephroureterectomy. TB infects the entire urinary tract, especially the ureter, the tube which connects the kidney to the bladder. The ureter's removal might be significant in this case.

KGB turned around in his seat with a shocked expression. No one but EJC would confront him, especially in public. He wiped the chocolate stain from his upper lip with his sleeve and stood quickly, facing the man. "Who licked the red off your candy, Elmer?" After KGB spoke, there was a significant pause as his words sank in. A quiet buzz began in the group as they understood the argumentative tone of the discussion. "Well, a simple nephrectomy is my understanding, Elmer. But Tara, answer the professor's question."

Tara moved down the aisle and took the microphone politely. She deliberated as she moved back to the front of the room. "A simple nephrectomy Dr. Crabb. There was no disease in the ureter. Anti-tuberculous drugs are on board to sterilize any unsuspected infection."

"Anti-tuberculous drugs? How completely cute. You will never cure him of his condition using those ineffective drugs. The ureter is the key, Dr. Patel. Aggressive surgery is the only answer. Are you not familiar with the pathogenesis of urinary kidney infections in tuberculosis? Read my article, Crabb et al., from the Journal in June 1943. Infection begins in the ureter. A stricture then forms, and the kidney becomes obstructed. TB bacterium then ascends to infect and form an abscess in the kidney. You'll never cure this pansy without taking the ureter. That's a fact, it is."

The issue was the surgical removal of a diseased ureter. If EJC was correct, the surgery left disease as a TB-infected ureter in the patient.

Nothing is more frightening for a surgeon than to have performed inadequate surgery, leaving disease behind. The urologic community now witnessed this issue out in the open. However, it was an uncomfortable confrontation, resulting in many audience members standing and leaving quietly.

EJC sat down slowly in his chair. There was a hush in the room. It was a historical fact that KGB and EJC were not friends. EJC was the former chairman of the vaunted urologic department at the UMC. A young and opportunistic urologist, Kenneth George Bolton, ousted him 20 years ago, and sparks have flown between them ever since. Perhaps the matching bow-ties were at fault.

KGB moved to the central aisle. He was foaming now, and he spit as he yelled. "You miserable old arrogant fart. You persnickety righteous fool. I should have rescinded your surgical privileges years ago. Why do we allow this ancient hack to continue to practice medicine?"

Dr. Crabb struggled to stand, then turned and shuffled to the back. A strangely satisfied smile broke over his face as he straightened his bowtie and fastened a button on his blazer. The professor looked Jackson Cooper directly in the eye and winked. He had difficulty opening the double doors, and the resident moved quickly to help the elderly man. As he walked away, his brogues clicked like keen crickets, and he said over his shoulder: "Fascinating debate, Dr. Bolton. The best of luck with him."

CHAPTER 4

"Hello, Mr. Latinsky. My name is Lisa. I'm a nursing student. I'm assigned to your case. Could I talk to you about your story?"

Lisa Waters was a UMC first-year nursing student. She possessed a memorable short blond bob haircut, and a kind, interested face that fascinated Maurice. The girl had a bright, friendly smile and brown caring eyes behind cute, red, round-framed glasses. Dressed in a starched white nursing outfit, a pink plastic stethoscope lay tossed behind her neck.

Maurice sat up slowly on the edge of his bed. With some help, he stood and moved to his bedside chair to talk. He was interested in telling his story to someone, and this nurse seemed willing to listen.

"What is it you want to ask me, dear?" Maurice finally felt awake this morning, and the promise of a listener pepped him right up. He seemed more robust today, feeling fresh and a little alive. He wondered if he was finally getting better. The girl interested him. He was a little excited, for he thought that talking to someone would distract from his Steve McQueen fantasies. Besides, he liked to talk, especially about himself.

"I want to know your story, Mr. Latinsky."

"Call me Maury, would you, dear? Mr. Latinsky is my dear late father."

Lisa whispered her response to the man. "Okay, but only to you, and quietly. My teacher, Ms. Crane, would disapprove of my using your first name, Mr. Latinsky. I mean Maury. It is sort of disrespectful, they say. But I don't care, do you? You prefer Maury to Maurice, Mr. Latinsky?"

"Only with friends, Lisa. With my friends, it is Maury. Otherwise, it's Maurice. May I consider you a friend?"

Lisa smiled and nodded yes.

Maurice told the girl everything he could remember.

The topic of conversation shifted to his visions. He knew they were delusions, but they were so real and disturbing. He was not sleeping well at all. The fevers were extremely disruptive and uncomfortable. The actual problem, however, was this continuing dream.

"What do you dream about, Maury?"

Maurice went on with his story. He was always Steve McQueen, dressed in green army fatigues. A German Nazi helmet sat on his closely cropped, balding head, a World War II vintage BMW motorcycle rumbling between his spindly legs. He would sit revving the engine, German soldiers in pursuit, and then launch himself over the barbed wire fence to freedom. The enemy goons occasionally captured him, but lately, he disappeared from the horde into the sunset and liberty.

Maurice felt comfortable talking to the girl. "I am him all the time, Lisa. Initially, only during sleep, like a dream at night. But now. Well, I think I am going crazy, dear. I feel like Steve McQueen over and over. Will I get better?"

Nurse Lisa was scribbling down notes on her clipboard. She paused and set her pen on the over-bed table. She poured Maurice a glass of water and encouraged him to drink. "Maury, it is just a fantasy. I know, but it must be troubling."

"I want to be free again, Lisa." His life was anything but free now. He continued with his story, appreciating the girl's interest. Hospitalized for over one month, continual medical care tortured him. He longed to return to Freddie, Suzette, his studio apartment, and his life as an interior decorator in Pacific Heights. Escape was always on his diminishingly capable brain. He just needed to figure out how.

He reviewed past events for the nurse. For months, he suffered from sores all over his skin, which refused to heal. There was a hacking and persistent cough. His hair fell out, and he had trouble with his gait and memory. He lost a lot of weight before the pain and fever brought him to the UMC's emergency room that one bleak night in May.

He remembered that evening so vividly. There was an unusual electrical thunderstorm with lightning. The storm-like event lit up the night sky in an eerie, foreboding manner as Freddie drove frantically to the hospital. He was shaking with fever, and sweat dripped from his brow. With his head aflame, he vomited in the back of their Ford Fairlane. Suzette tried to comfort him. The dog was concerned, quietly licking his hands and face with love.

First, he met Dr. Patel, who seemed to run things. She was very competent, attractive in a female sort of way. She eventually told him that infection with the Human Immunodeficiency Virus, or HIV, was ravaging his body. Then it was the diagnosis of Acquired Immune Deficiency Syndrome or AIDS. She informed him about the tuberculosis in his right kidney and the need for its removal. There was the lengthy surgery and seemingly endless hospital abuse. His dreams began soon after. Unable to meet Lisa's gaze, tears welled in his eyes.

The Great Escape plagued his sleeping hours. He only saw the movie once. It was in a lovely Indie style theatre in San Francisco. Freddie was with him, and they ate popcorn and Raisinets while they watched a story of a World War II prisoner who longed to escape. They drank from a bottle of fine California Pinot Noir, wrapped in a brown paper bag, while they snuggled on the balcony. They barely watched the film. That jump scene, however, must have made an impression. While dreams of it plagued his sleep of late, he was seeing it in his brain nonstop.

"How are you feeling today, Maury?" To this point, the young nurse was primarily silent, fascinated, and taking feverish notes on her clipboard. She kept pouring the man water and encouraging him to drink. "It is important for you, Maury. The water will flush out the infection, I think."

"Thank you, dear." Maurice took a long drink and wiped his mouth with his hand. He felt surprised.

"Today, I feel strong. It is all because of you, dear. You are interested in me. I appreciate that."

The girl stood, slightly embarrassed, gazing at the wall clock. "Maury, I have to go now. I'll visit you daily during this rotation. Would you like that?"

"Dear, I look forward to your return."

Lisa smiled. She touched Maurice's forehead, turned, and left the room. Maurice was very coherent that day. In the future, he would have fewer and fewer times like that. He suffered from HIV dementia, and it was progressing; his condition was not improving. The story of The Great Escape would continue to dominate his life.

•   •   •   •   •

He felt himself the vaunted cooler king, Captain Virgil Hilts, the person behind the Steve McQueen character. The soldier in the movie was continuously escaping the Stalag. He was constantly sneaking off rendezvousing with his lover in the local hamlet. The movie's soldier continuously got caught and sent back to jail for punishment. For him, the escape was the goal.

McQueen's character was quite a role model for Maurice Latinsky. The patient dreamed about him. Escape was also Maurice's obsession, and as his psychopathology and dementia progressed, this fanciful delusion took over.

It started when he could drink nothing after surgery. The urinal was available, and he was so thirsty. Now the urine drinking was only occasionally. He would see the urinal and feel drawn to the warm fluid within. At first, the doctors didn't allow him to drink water, but sometimes he felt an overpowering urge to consume this fluid. He began to get power in his mind from this activity. He would need that to escape.

Maurice was obsessed with escaping the hospital and returning to his former life. He must escape, he thought. It was so overpowering. The repetitive notion of escape, destination, and companionship plagued the man day and night, filling his mind with unanswered questions.

The large window in his room loomed as a possibility. He tried to open it once without the nurses knowing. It was big enough but bolted shut and not operable. Through the window, it looked like he was on the second floor, high above the ground. The window was not the answer. Could he just run down the hall? His immobility and the staff made it impossible.

Standing up against the wall in the hallway was a curious possibility. It was a supply cart, a handcart in the hall, with supplies needed for the daily nurses' chores. Stocked on the wagon were gauze, IV fluids bags and tubing, band-aids, disposable scissors and suture trays, culture tubes, sterile towels, and other supplies. Linen curtains covered the carts, hanging to the floor and obstructing the view of their contents. When the staff needed an item, they lifted the curtain and grabbed the article. Big mobile wheels allowed the cart to be moved with ease.

The supply cart sat in the hallway, ready for the nurse's use. The supply room stored stocked replacements and used-up carts. Eventually, someone pushed the empty carts down the hall to the basement. It was worth a try; Maurice decided on a day.

He dressed that morning in hospital-issued pajamas. They were thin white cotton with barely visible blue pinstripes. He wore a light cardigan sweater and tossed on a warmer hospital robe, concealing this. On his feet were his only choice: hospital-issued white slippers. He had only one twenty-dollar bill on his nightstand and wadded it up in his back pocket, unsure of the future. He took along his only photo of Freddie, himself, and Suzette.

As was his practice, Freddie rang him that morning on the phone. He wanted to chat to assess his mental status for the day. Maurice talked briefly, trying not to reveal his plan. His partner would not arrive until tonight, allowing him time to act on his plot.

Maurice's periods of clarity were dwindling. He was aware of the fact and tried to face reality. He chose a morning when he would be fresh and alone during the nurse's morning report. Here staff were absent for 15 minutes to discuss ward and patients. This timing would give him a brief chance to escape.

He slipped onto the empty supply cart in the supply room. Maurice was naturally small. However, he was now outright tiny, weighing just 82 pounds. Maurice could slide into an empty cart, close the curtains, and wait. As the carriage moved and entered the eastern elevator, he sensed a breakthrough.

He lay in central supply for what seemed like hours. At first, there was activity around him. He was afraid that someone would open the curtains and discover him. Things, however, are slow in a large hospital, and no one ever notices. Eventually, the silence became continuous, a signal that he was in the clear.

Maurice quietly rolled out of the cart. When his feet touched the floor and he was upright, the man felt lightheaded with dizziness. When the feeling passed, he looked around. In a sizable room, he found many empty carts. The lights were overpowering after hours in the dark. Maurice moved to the wall switch and doused them.

Maurice was unclear about his location in the hospital. He thought he had gone down two floors when in the elevator. Fear tinged his gaze as he surveyed the room. A door opened silently, unveiling a long hallway that vanished in both directions. Stocked carts and ventilators lined the walls.

He decided on a direction and walked down the hallway. Soon there were double doors that opened automatically. Having passed them, he turned and proceeded down another hallway. Two scrub suit-wearing employees with stretchy surgical hats walked by the man. They were talking among themselves and passed Maurice without even a look. The cafeteria sign hung on the wall. It encouraged him, for he now knew his way out.

•   •   •   •   •

She was sitting in the cafeteria when Maurice Latinsky entered through a side door. He recognized her immediately, her bob haircut so memorable. Lisa Waters sat at a table, eating lunch and talking to a few fellow students. Brief eye contact with the girl startled Maurice. His heart started racing. Was he caught? He swiftly turned and walked through the glass doors.

Lisa was concerned with Maurice's presence in the cafeteria alone. She stood, excused herself, moved across the room, and looked out through the doors. He was sitting on a small bench in the enclosed patio. He seemed relaxed under the sun. She had mixed emotions, feeling some sadness for the man. Reluctantly, Lisa picked up the phone on the wall and paged the intern on the service.

"Doctor Nelson, Mr. Latinsky, is down here alone in the cafeteria. He appears content, lounging in the sun on the patio near the back doors. I am worried about him. I don't think he should be down here alone, do you?"

"How did he get there? The head nurse, Cecelia, just paged me. He disappeared from the ward during the morning report. His Rifampin dose is due. I'll come down, Lisa. Please watch him; he is not supposed to be out alone, especially in the sun. Rifampin is phototoxic, you know."

The sun was glorious, and so welcomed that day in June 1983. Maurice did not care or know about Rifampin, a tuberculosis antibiotic. There was a clean smell of flowers and a warm and wonderful sun. Maurice sat on the wooden bench, basking in the light and stretching his exhausted legs. He was himself now, his Steve McQueen character nowhere in sight. His thinking was so clear, and Maurice realized that the ward tormented him. However, he was out of ideas. The patio stood enclosed by buildings, free of exits other than to return through the cafeteria. Lisa was there, and he felt uneasy. He was free, but not ultimately.

Dr. Nelson and Dr. Cooper showed up quickly. Jackson sat next to Maurice. "Beautiful day, isn't it, Mr. Latinsky? How did you get down here?"

Maurice smiled sadly at the resident. "I flew, Dr. Cooper. I must say, it is wonderful down here."

"But Maurice, you shouldn't be out here alone. Don't you realize you need fluids?"

"Dr. Cooper. I am tired. I am not sure I can walk back."

Michael wheeled a black leather wheelchair to the patient's side. Maurice stood with help, annoying but necessary. They departed the patio and returned to the ward.

CHAPTER 5

Eleanor Grubb entered the urology department, her verve in full swing. She set her sights on everyone and anyone, indicting them on charges of anything. She was a round woman, diminutive but moderately plump and hovering at 93 years of age. Eleanor possessed a wrinkled, sallow face with drooping jowls adorned with the generous use of pasty makeup. The woman wore a pink and blue wrap-around floral house dress and sauntered on black lace-up, common sense, oxford shoes with a low spooled heel. With determination and a strong sense of entitlement, she marched down the hallway.

What distinguished the woman was a huge, black tote bag purse she carried over her shoulder. It was full of papers, and lipstick, and who knows what else. The bag was her weapon of choice, and she would swing it with authority, rebuking anyone.

Jackson Cooper was in the urology library with his nose in a recent journal. An article on surgical handling of the ureter in infectious conditions had grabbed his attention, given the recent scuffle in grand rounds. When she entered, Jackson suspected an ambush.

Mrs. Grubb announced her presence with a firm chuck of her purse into the open library door. She intended to proclaim herself and draw Jackson's attention. Identify yourself, would-be acolyte. "The toilet needs some attention."

Eleanor's question was a continuation of her abuse of the house staff. She literally felt that they were servants and housekeepers. The resident looked up and smiled a tired smile. His mind went to his interaction with Dr. Elmer Grubb. Two for the ages, he thought, as a horrified image of the couple in a romantic liaison flashed over his exhausted brain.

"Well, Mrs. Grubb, you look well today. I am Jackson, Jackson Cooper. We met at Dr. Bolton's tea and pastry event. I am a resident for your husband."

"Don't disparage me, Jack. Where is the old sloth? Are you the one who wouldn't eat his birthday cupcake?"

While his name was Jackson, the name Jack brought a loathing to his mind. All his life, people would shorten his name. He never liked the nickname. Why confront the old bag? He thought to himself.

"Dr. Grubb is in his office, I think. Mrs. Grubb, I ate the cupcake Saturday. It was delicious." In reality, it was horrible. It was stale and tasted like a beet-flavored fig pastry. He tossed it after one bite. Jackson rose with trepidation. He left, passing her through the door. "Mrs. Grubb, let me take you to him."

"Sit down. I know the way better than you." She swung her purse and hit the resident on his backside. "Can't a girl get a cup of tea around here, Jack?" Jackson grinned a controlled smile. "I will bring you one in Dr. Crabb's office."

Jackson stood tentatively at the same heavy wooden door and wondered if he should turn around and leave. Upon his knock, a crackly voice invited him inside.

The air smelled old and stale again. Across the room, two ancient people sat in matching brown leather armchairs, separated by a round-topped wooden table with an antique lamp that flickered as if old. They were laughing and quietly talking like two newly found paramours.

"Bubba, we have a get-together with the Michaels on Saturday. You should wear your nice cardigan sweater I gave you at Christmas." Eleanor was bubbling with respect and admiration. The air was almost thick with sickening insincerity.

Jackson took the cup of tea and set it on the table. He placed a sugar bag and a creamer near her cup. He brought a cup for the professor as well.

"Three sugars, Jack. I always use three. What is going on in your little pea brain?" The woman picked up the sugars and dumped them unceremoniously into the cup.

"I like my tea black, Jack. You know, like I like my women." The two antique creatures guffawed like Rodney Dangerfield was doing standup. The professor responded to his wife. "The cardigan will be marvelous, Bubbie."

Jackson stood uncomfortably. The two jackals weighed on his mind. Another image of a romantic liaison crashed across his consciousness. He might vomit.

Once in the library, Jackson crashed, plopping down on a chair. Still tentative and anxious, he remembered his torment was not over. Sometime Jackson must talk to the professor about this journal article. He would wait until Eleanor left for the evening.

He heard the door to the girl's bathroom close with a crash. With no acknowledgement, she walked past the library. As she disappeared down the hallway, Jackson realized something was wrong. A string of wet toilet paper hung over her rear, rolling out her pantyhose and dangling to the back of her knees. Pulled up in the back was her dress, revealing a wrinkled pantyhose covered backside. She pranced along on her low-heeled oxfords, unaware of her humiliating mistake.

Jackson forever replaced the previous distressing romantic images of the couple with this last sight in his brain. Karma. Karma always strikes, thought the content resident.

•   •   •   •   •

Maurice Latinsky was not doing well. His fevers persisted each night, and his delusional behavior was progressing. On morning rounds, Dr. Patel and the others discussed his case.

"Mike, how is Mr. Latinsky doing this morning?"

"He has nightly fevers. His high-temperature last night was 103. Jackson was on call, and he had them get blood and urine cultures and give him Tylenol. I am concerned, Tara. He has a small red pustule just below his incision. Maybe it is a small abscess that we could I/D." The intern presented that the patient had a red lesion below his incision. If it was a skin abscess, it could be the source of his fever. He proposed incising the lesion, hoping to drain away the infection.

Tara looked at Jackson, interested in his input. "He is still fantasizing and delusional. The escape to the cafeteria was merely a sign. We need to CAT scan his head. Maybe he has a TB or Toxoplasmosis abscess in the brain, Tara." Jackson was concerned about an infection in the patient's brain. Toxoplasmosis is a parasite and a common AIDS-related infection. If Maurice had an abscess in the brain, it would explain his fevers and confusion.

"Dr. Patel, he is still drinking his urine." Julie was his overnight nurse. She caught him at midnight drinking from his urinal. "He does it just rarely, but it worries me."

"Could it be a source of his delusions? I read an article in the journal once that listed hallucinations as a result of the oral intake of urine." Jackson was just throwing out some information and thoughts. Few patients drink their urine, none of the Dr.'s were familiar with similar cases. Urine is full of electrolytes and toxins, especially potassium. In addition, medications appear in the urine. Those on desert islands have difficulty with this behavior.

Tara looked at the group with frustration. "Julie, keep the urinal away from him."

"I tried, Dr., but he can't get to the bathroom to void. He has to use a urinal. He had it to his mouth before I could do anything. Do you really think it is causing his visions?"

"I doubt it. But it isn't good for him. I like the idea of a brain infection. Let's get a CAT scan, Mike." Tara spoke for the group, dictating directions to the intern. She motioned for them to enter Maurice's room.

Maurice was asleep, laying on his back, moist sheets crumbled up at his feet. When the group appeared at the bedside, Maurice woke with a growl, startled by their presence. He opened his heterochromatic eyes and stared at Tara with a vacant gaze.

"Mr. Latinsky, how are you this morning?" Maurice smiled, saying nothing. Tara looked at the patient's abdominal incision and noticed a red, round, raised bump below it. The bump looked like a pustule filled with pus. "Is that tender, Mr. Latinsky?"

Maurice was silent. He shook his head yes.

"Good observation, Mike. Get an I/D kit, a culture tube, and some Lidocaine. Do it at the bedside."

What happened next became a fabled story at UMC. The doctor applied Lidocaine and made a small incision. Immediately, foul, thick pus squirted from the wound and hit the intern in the chest. The wound drained prolifically. It drained and drained and drained, first filling the bedside and then flowing onto and across the floor. Mike grabbed a trash can to catch the discharge. Liquid overflowed from the can and spilled onto the floor. The smell was horrific; the pus disgusting. It covered the group's shoes as the river of pus made its way to the hallway door.

Horror spread among the group. Some became nauseated. They exited the room, shrieking and trying to avoid the freeway of pus. Soon, a crowd came rushing. Nurses and staff brought mops and buckets, wondering about the origin of the horrific smell. It wafted through the door, spread to the hallway, and eventually, throughout the hospital. They opened windows, deployed fans, and scrubbed and disinfected the floor. UMC smelled for weeks. Maurice Latinsky had a problem.

CHAPTER 6

Wei Huan was a 47-year-old Asian male. In 1961, at 24, he underwent a hemicorpectomy to treat locally widespread, invasive penile cancer. First described in 1951, the surgery involved the amputation of the pelvis and lower extremities by transection of the lumbar spine and cord, aorta, and inferior vena cava. Surgeons in Detroit performed the first such surgery in 1960. This patient lived for just ten days. Thereafter, the procedure was a rare and extremely morbid operation with a mortality of 50 percent.

Wei was the surgery's first patient at UMC. A multidisciplinary surgical team performed the complicated procedure, including orthopedic, urologic, neurosurgical, general surgeons, and anesthesiologists. Dr. Elmer Crabb was the urologist and continued being the patient's urologic physician.

Details of the surgery included the construction of a colostomy for bowel evacuation and an ileal conduit for urinary excretion. Here, the surgeon brings portions of the bowel to the skin as stomas, allowing bowel and urinary waste to drain into bags.

Jackson Cooper knocked quietly on the door and entered the exam room. He didn't expect Wei Huan. The patient stood on the exam table, the lower edge of his body devoid of legs and pelvis, encased in a rubber-padded bucket. He dressed in a hospital-issued gown and had black, well-groomed hair, long, stringy sideburns, and a thin blackish mustache. To his right stood a two-foot square wooden push board with small skate-type wheels, turned on its side and leaning against the wall.

"Hi Doc, where is the little man?" Wei shook Jackson's outstretched hand as he questioned where Dr. Elmer Crabb was.

"He is over in his office. After we talk and examine you, I will get him. How are you, Mr. Huan? I see you have a slight fever this morning."

"Yes. A fever. Week-long fevers. And there is blood and some crud in my urine bag. Just like before." With his hands on the table, Wei struggled and lifted himself out of the bucket. He set it on the floor by his board and lay on his back. "Sorry, Doc, I don't feel so well."

"Let me see." Jackson pulled up the patient's gown, exposing the rest of his abdomen. On his lower left side hung a colostomy bag containing dark stool. On the right, another bag, this one filled with blood-tinged urine. Jackson examined his abdomen. He pushed on his belly and asked if he was tender. Yes, Wei signaled under the left ribs. "Stones? Do you think you have one again?"

Wei struggled and sat up on the table. He spoke quietly with resignation. "Ya, I guess so. I always get them on that side. I hurt in the back, too."

Jackson tapped his back over his left flank. Wei flinched with pain. "We haven't seen you in a few years, Mr. Huan. Let's get an x-ray immediately."

Wei reached and retrieved his bucket, slipping it over his abdominal stump. "So, go downstairs? Will they let me bring the x-ray back here?" The patient was utterly familiar with the hospital routine and the hospital layout. He was famous at UMC, a tragic-looking man on a skate-wheeled board.

"Yes, but we have an x-ray machine in the clinic now. It is over by the receptionist. Oscar, the x-ray tech, will help you."

Wei tied his gown in the back around his abdomen and chest. He reached the floor for his board and tossed it onto the ground. He lifted his body and set himself down on the board. Jackson kindly opened the door for him.

Jackson sat in the conference room, writing notes and reviewing patient charts.

"Doctor, here is Mr. Huan's KUB." Oscar was a young Filipino male x-ray technician. He handed Jackson a kidney ureter and bladder film, or KUB.

The resident took the film and snapped it up onto an x-ray view box. "Oh boy," Jackson said sadly. On the film was a huge staghorn-shaped stone overlying the left kidney.

Wei had a problem. He had an ileal conduit, or "loop." Here, a piece of bowel was hooked to his two kidney ureters, with the other end brought out to the skin as a stoma. His urine then drained into the stoma bag. As was typical of loops, stones formed. His last episode was five years ago. A gigantic stone, resembling a staghorn, occupied his kidney.

Jackson trudged across the hall. He stopped in the resident's office for some mental reinforcement. He opened the old Percocet prescription bottle for security and smelled the residual contents. Jackson then shook out and downed two Tic Tacs. Memories of his past drug use flooded his continually tempted, addict brain.

Jackson stood tentatively at the same heavy wooden door and knocked. He heard the typical crackly response. "Come in."

Again, Jackson was aware of the old, cold, stale air. The professor sat at his desk, typing away feverishly on an ancient black Corona mechanical typewriter. A cup of tea sat to his right, a large stack of typed pages to his left. Dr. Crabb remained engrossed in his work. "Speak up, Dr. Cooper. What did that KUB show?"

"Can I put it on your view box, Dr. Crabb?" Jackson crossed the room and snapped the film up on the box.

The professor stood slowly. He shuffled across the room. "For Pete's sake, Dr. Cooper, where is his previous film? You never examine a KUB without the prior film. He was clean of stones in 1978. Let's see the film."

Luckily, Jackson had the old film. He snapped it up on the box.

Dr. Crabb pulled out a telescoping pointer pen from his coat pocket. "A pointer. I don't trust someone who doesn't carry a pointer, Dr. Cooper. Invest in one. Now, this 1978 film shows we cleaned him out of stones." The professor waved his silver pointer over the old film like a conductor. He began pointing at the new film. "Now, here is a big booger. A full staghorn, and I bet he has blood, pus, and fever, right?"

"Yes, Dr. Crabb. For about a week."

The professor slid shut his pointer and put it in his coat. He turned and returned to his desk. He began typing again. "Does that Chink still scoot around on a board?"

Jackson silently stood, gazing at the man. This ethnic slur was especially disturbing for the resident. His best friend in medical school was Asian. Oh well, the professor was a well-known, ancient, insensitive bigot. Nothing the man said surprised Jackson. He disregarded the professor's question. "What do we do about the staghorn?"

The professor looked up from his typing. He then referred to the urologic literature. "Read your Campbell's, *Textbook of Urology*. Peruse James F. Glenn's *Urologic Surgery* text. Oh, and how about reading Crabb and Edwards, October, volume 89 of the 1962 Journal? We will perform an anatrophic nephrolithotomy, of course. We'll do it on Friday morning. Admit him now and get him prepared, Dr. Cooper. Tell Dr. Patel that rather than her, you will assist me personally."

•   •   •   •   •

"We need to hurry to get your CAT scan, Mr. Latinsky." Mike Nelson pushed a wheelchair through the lobby to the radiology suite. The transportation people were late, so the intern wheeled him to his appointment. The doctor ordered a CAT scan of the head and abdomen for 2 p.m. He would just make it.

Jim, the tech, grabbed the wheelchair and quickly wheeled Maurice away. The CAT scan operator was Mike's friend. It helps to have friends when you are an intern.

The x-ray lobby was empty, and Mike waited for Maurice. He took his clipboard, sat next to the phone, made several calls, and scanned his notes.

Soon, something startled him. "Mike! Mike! Stop using the phone," the tech urgently said. "Mr. Mr. Latinsky is gone."

"What do you mean, gone, Jim?"

The technician looked concerned, exacerbated, and frantically waving his arms. "He's just gone. The strangest thing happened. Lights in the scanner abruptly turned off. It was pitch dark for just a minute. When they went on, Mr. Latinsky was gone."

•　　•　　•　　•　　•

It was a beautiful summer day when Maurice wandered out the front doors of the UMC. There was a peaceful duck pond with water fountains spraying high in the air and a nice bench for a visitor to sit. Wearing hospital attire, he wasn't the only patient enjoying the view. Maurice was gradually calming down. His day was turning around. He felt the ducks were lucky.

Wei was being admitted to the hospital that afternoon. He was scooting along the walkway after gathering his belongings from his handicapped van on his way to admitting. Something caused him to stop, scoot up to the fountains, and rest momentarily.

Maurice walked up and sat next to the scooter-bound man. His mind was clearer this afternoon, his escape from the CAT scanner a quirky twist of fate that woke him from a deep delusional dream. Wei looked at Maurice, and Maurice looked at Wei. Here was a brutally disabled man who occupied a scooter board, standing on the stump of his belly. Maurice was a severely wasted and obviously ill man. The two instantly related.

"What happened to you?" Maurice wondered shyly.

"Cancer, and you?"

"I have AIDS. It is in my immune system."

"What are you doing out here? Don't you need to be in the hospital?" For much of Wei's adult life, UMC was his fate. He knew Maurice was very sick. Maurice appeared wasted, with red and swollen gums and stubble for hair. The man didn't belong at the fountains. Wei was heading for another huge surgery on Friday. He sensed that a similar fate awaited his new friend.

Maurice realized Wei was right. It was uncomfortable, but the hospital and its staff were trying to treat him. He stood and strolled toward the hospital, with Wei on his board, scooting alongside. "Come on. Let's go inside."

CHAPTER 7

Jackson Cooper was busy in the nursing station, completing his morning hospital progress notes. He needed to finish, check on labs, and then start a challenging IV on an obese woman. Then the resident was due in Lee W.'s urology clinic. Starving and pressed for time, he rarely had lunch. He debated his options. In his coat pocket was a day-old peanut butter sandwich or he could run to the cafeteria. He had mixed feelings. Save time with the sandwich or suffer another dreadful meal in the cafeteria? The page to his beeper decided it for him.

"This is Dr. Cooper. I was paged."

"Hi Jackson, it is Patrice. How are you? Can we meet in the cafeteria? I have a few minutes, I think." Patrice Summers was Jackson's good friend. She was a second-year plastic surgery resident who completed her surgery internship last year with Jackson. Jackson hoped they were more than just friends. The girl was with him throughout that troubling year. She resuscitated him after his Fentanyl overdose. So romantic! She, too, was a Christian, but their church life of late was lacking. Were they destined to be together? He wondered. It was the hospital, their rotations, and their call schedules, all confounding factors in the life of UMC residents.

She was sitting at their table when Jackson arrived. The cafeteria comprised circular tables arranged in a large open room, with a stainless-steel counter and cafeteria workings along the east end. Their table faced the wall where a wall phone hung, which was convenient for obvious reasons.

Patrice was again letting her brown hair grow. Her bleached streak over her forehead was once again present. Jackson complimented the girl. He was a fan of it. When they first met last year, Patrice was wearing the distinctive streak. Her dark green eyes always fascinated him. They were so appealing to the man. Yes, Jackson missed Patrice. Did the girl miss him?

Jackson reached into her coat pocket and retrieved her pack of Winstons. "Still not smoking?"

Patrice laughed. She smoked cigarettes in the past during medical school. Now she just carried a pack for comfort. It was one of the first quirky things that Jackson remembered about the girl.

"I am on surgery B again. Not much plastics. You know, appys, choles, gunshot wounds, the usual. What are you doing, Jackson?" As she spoke about appendectomies and cholecystectomies, she got a page on her beeper. Patrice looked at Jackson sheepishly. "Sorry, I'm covering the ER."

The two stood. Jackson tried quickly to tell her of the exciting news. "Crabb says I get to do an anatrophic nephrolithotomy on Friday. My chief is jealous. Answer your page, Patrice."

The nephrolithotomy was a surgical coup for the second-year urology resident. Contrary to protocol, EJC insisted that Jackson, a junior resident, rather than the chief resident, Tara Patel, would do the nephrolithotomy. Jackson sensed some jealous sensitivity from the woman. However, she ultimately encouraged him and suggested an article to read.

When Patrice returned to the table, Jackson found her attention divided. She gathered her purse, clipboard, and grabbed the pack of Winstons from the table. "A gunshot wound to the face in the ER. Suicide attempt. Sorry, Jackson, I got to go."

•　　　•　　　•　　　•　　　•

Maurice Latinsky had his CAT scan the same day as his duck pond revelation. He had disappeared from the hospital after the power outage. His location was unknown to the staff. On his return to the ward, he was strangely calm. He slept the rest of the day. He ate an unusually large portion of his meal. He was not coveting his urine. His fevers were silent, and he wasn't speaking of Steve McQueen and escape.

Mike Nelson retrieved the CAT scan films from radiology to present them the following day at the departmental meeting in the urology library. The entire department, other than EJC, attended these twice-weekly meetings. Here, the team would present and discuss each patient on the service.

Kenneth George Bolton arrived and sat in his usual chair at the front of the room. He ordered a cup of C from the intern, delivered steaming hot. KGB was angry this morning, but the Southern man didn't care why. "Why is a DeNano tube in the lady? What's her name? Cramstein?"

A suprapubic tube was a urinary drainage catheter placed directly through the skin in the lower abdomen and into the bladder. KGB's design, the Bolton tube, was bulky and difficult to place. The house staff preferred the DeNano tube. It was easier and more functional.

Jackson's answer was straightforward. "Mrs. Cranston, it is Cranston, Dr. Bolton," he said, correcting the man's recollection of often wrong names. "OR has no Bolton tubes left. I might find one around UMC. Do you want me to change out the tube, Dr. Bolton?"

KGB just reddened up with resignation. He wanted to pounce on someone this morning. He noisily slurped his chocolate and shook his head in refusal. "Jack, for future reference, the Bolton tube is the best choice."

"Mr. Latinsky is a 37-year-old white male with HIV/AIDS and tuberculosis abscesses in his right kidney." Mike was standing at the room's front, beginning the conference with patient presentations. "He is post-op from a right simple nephrectomy but has a persistent fever, confusion, and drainage. Here are the CAT scans obtained just yesterday."

Tara stood and moved to the view box. "You see, this patient has progressive dementia with a delusional overlay." She pulled a pointer from her coat and pointed. "This CAT scan of his head, however, is free of abscesses and looks okay. Because of his fever and an incisional pustule, we I/Ded the lesion. The hospital knows that prolific quantities of foul pus drained from the wound. Mike, do we know what the pus grew?"

Mike turned to Jackson. "Did you run by the infectious disease lab?"

"*Mycobacterium kansasii*, a TB bug seen only in AIDS and HIV." Jackson had never seen or heard of such an infection, the most common TB bacterium being Mycobacterium tuberculii.

Tara took the abdominal scan from the intern. She pulled down the head CAT scan and snapped up the belly views. With her pointer, she outlined areas on the scan. "Note the absent right kidney. There is an abscess attached to the stump of the right ureter. This is where Mr. Latinsky's fever is coming from."

"The ureteral stump was always the key, you clowns." Elmer J. Crabb, professor emeritus, appeared at the library door. He had a strangely satisfied look on his otherwise crabby face. "A nephroureterectomy. Always perform a nephroureterectomy in renal TB. Whose brilliant decision was this? Why was this just a simple nephrectomy? Do any of you jokers read the literature?"

KGB dropped his cup of C on the carpet floor and jumped up in defense. "Why, you ignorant old fool. This isn't 1945. Surgery has changed you dup. Drugs, we have drugs now, Elmer. You never admitted that, you little bent over buffoon."

Tara moved to calm the chairman, who was red, huffing, and stomping his feet. The man was extremely angry. "Dr. Bolton, we need to re-explore Mr. Latinsky. We should go back and extract the ureter to drain the abscess. It is straightforward. We need to do it soon."

EJC turned and shuffled off, his brogues clicking like a keen cricket. Again, a sly smile was on his twisted face. "A positively brilliant conclusion, class."

•　　•　　•　　•　　•

Wei Huan slept poorly through the night. He woke up on Friday at five a.m. A cute female nurse shaved his abdomen. She changed his colostomy and urinary bags for new ones. The nurse then scrubbed him with ice-cold iodine-containing liquid. She placed a surgical hat on his head.

Maurice Latinsky was awake as well. He knew of the impending surgery for his newfound friend. He crawled from bed, wrapped himself in a white cotton bathrobe, and slipped on hospital-issue slippers. His urinal stood calling him. He chose to ignore it. He padded down the hallway and slipped into Wei's room.

Wei was reading his Bible. He set it down and smiled at his friend. "You came just like you said, Maury. Thank you, my friend."

"Do you think you will be back here this afternoon, Wei?"

"No, they said something about the ICU. It is on the third floor, just above us. Visit me tonight. That is if you can, Maury."

CHAPTER 8

A frantic hysteria overwhelmed the crash room as Patrice arrived in the emergency department. A young black male attempted to kill himself with a 12-gauge pump-action shotgun. Something about lover's scorn, something about money, of course. He propped the gun butt between his knees; the barrel lodged under his chin. The blast carved off the front of his face, chin, jaw, tongue, nose, and eyeball in a meat grinder fashion. Though his life continued, his journey towards medical tragedy and torture began.

A frenetic beehive characterized ER room one, as the staff struggled with the man's life. Anesthesia was helplessly trying to intubate him, with impossible attempts at gaining access to his airway through his absent mouth and nose. A surgeon was busy at the neck, furiously trying to perform a tracheostomy. There was a call for blood hung on poles as the man exsanguinated, his fluids flying everywhere. Briefly, the team performed CPR, as his tired heart also tried to stop. His feet shot up into the air using the Trendelenburg position.

Patrice wanted a chance to help. The man needed a Foley urinary catheter, and she grabbed a catheter tray and worked. But the patient had severe phimosis, a tight, constrictive ring of scar in his penile foreskin, which prevented access to his urethral opening. No way, she thought. Patrice could not pass the catheter.

Her mind returned to the cafeteria and Jackson Cooper. She knew the urologist could quickly remedy the situation. "Jackson, we need help in the crash room. Could you do a dorsal slit and pass a Foley? You'd be such a hero. For you, I know it is simple. I've never even seen one done."

Jackson decided that Lee W.'s clinic would have to wait. He picked up his things and rushed to the ER. On the way, he grabbed a circumcision kit, catheters, and a minor surgery tray. On a lark, Jackson grabbed a suprapubic catheter tray. It was the DeNano tube Bolton hated.

Mayhem continued in the crash room. People scoured over the critical patient. There was rushing and yelling as Jackson and Patrice tried to clean his groin.

Phimosis occurs when the foreskin is too tight to expose the glans or urethral opening. Jackson dropped his instrument trays on the man's lower abdomen. Patrice took a squirt bottle of iodine soap and soaked his genital area.

"Here you do this, Patrice." Jackson wanted her to learn on the job. He handed her a sterile clamp and a pair of scissors. As the saying goes, in a teaching institution, it is: *see one procedure, do one procedure, then teach one.* Here was an example of that idiom.

Patrice took a straight hemostat clamp and crimped the site of the intended foreskin incision to stop any bleeding. A quick cut with the scissors opened the foreskin, revealing the glans and urethra. "Here, Jackson, take over."

Jackson took a Foley and attempted to pass the catheter. Despite attempts, the catheter could not advance past the mid-penis. The man faced another issue—a urethral stricture blocking the tube's passage. The patient needed a catheter in the urinary tract to monitor his urinary output. He would have to forget the Foley catheter for the time. How to get urine drainage was another question.

A suprapubic catheter is a tube inserted through the abdominal skin into the bladder. The urinary output can then be measurable. Jackson opened and installed the DeBano suprapubic tube with just a few maneuvers. Clear, fresh urine draining into a bag on the floor was the result.

KGB financially benefited from the use of his namesake product, the Bolton suprapubic tube. However, it was bulky and difficult to use. House staff rarely used the device. The chairman would be disappointed in Jackson's use of the competitor's product. He hoped KGB would not find out.

●　　　●　　　●　　　●　　　●

Kenneth George Bolton could not bring himself to re-operate on Maurice Latinsky. The sticky issue was his ureteral stump and abscess, retained after his prior surgery. KGB, in actuality, agreed with EJC. The kidney and ureter should have been removed together, called a nephroureterectomy. However, he hated Crabb, his attitude, and the confrontation. He hated his appearance, age, grumpiness, and attitude. The chairman was just a slight bit jealous of the professor's steely reputation in the urologic community. He would not acknowledge the correct avenue, or his incorrect decision, in this patient. KGB asked Lee W. Hickok to be the surgical attending.

Tara Patel just wanted to begin the case. She knew a mistake had been made. She recognized it was responsible for some of Maurice's adverse course. Draining pus at the bedside resulted from incomplete surgery. His fevers, as well as his delusional behavior, were likely the result. The patient would not improve without this salvage procedure.

Re-exploring an abdomen after a prior surgery was like encountering a site of a bomb detonation. The preceding surgery leaves the abdomen as a war zone. Intense adhesions, swelling, and scarring make the dissection necessary in the procedure challenging.

That is what was found at surgery. Identifying and removing the ureter was nearly impossible. Tracing it down to the bladder was quite difficult. The surrounding abdominal contents were stuck, inflamed, edematous, and friable. Tuberculous pus hid in pockets everywhere.

After the six-hour procedure, Tara Patel and Lee W. Hickok adjourned to Lee W.'s office. Tara and Lee W. both plopped into chairs in the cramped room.

"I am glad that is over." Tara removed her cap and took a long drink from a bottle of icy water. She chewed a stick of string cheese for sustenance. She looked exhausted.

"Oh, my gosh. That was awful, y'all. I need a shot of sweet amber. Oh ya, I am an alcoholic, and I, unfortunately, am sober. Too bad." Lee W. stood and pulled his shoe covers off his cowboy boots and tossed them on the floor. He pulled his perspiration-soaked scrub top over his head and covered up with his white coat. In the adjacent kitchen sink, he washed his face and neck and wet back his hair. "Jackson and Mike will have their hands full in the ICU tonight."

Tara was concerned about the stability of Maurice Latinsky over the next 24 hours. He lost a great deal of blood. He received massive amounts of blood and fluids. The duration of his anesthesia was lengthy, and he needed a significant amount of time on the ventilator. Also, Maurice was unwell. He suffered from immune compromise, ravaged by AIDS. He had lost over 50 pounds in the last year. His nutrition was poor. These factors predicted a rocky post-operative course for the man.

• • • • •

Jackson Cooper stood at Maurice's bedside. He looked at the monitors and adjusted his IV rate. Looking at the bags of drugs hanging, the resident seemed satisfied. Jackson turned when he heard the familiar scooting sound. Wei Huan was behind him, shuffling over the floor on his board.

"Wei, what are you doing here?" He had a pole with an IV attached to his board.

"Dr. Cooper. How is the patient doing?"

"Well, he had an extensive surgery. He is stable, however. We will just have to follow him. It won't be easy for him."

Jackson excused himself. He left the room to answer his page. Wei scooted to the bedside. The patient lay on his back, puffing away on the ventilator. "Maurice, can you hear me? You are doing okay. Open your eyes if you can."

When Maurice's eyelids popped open, it frightened Wei. Only then did he notice his eyes were heterochromatic. The green and blue irises were shiny and awake. Maurice lifted his hand and squeezed his friend's. Maurice was back.

CHAPTER 9

The night loomed as a thrilling respite from the daily grind of UMC oppression and medical tyranny. Jackson Cooper looked at himself in the mirror with anticipation. He was shaving with a dull OR prep razor in the communal male lavatory of the call room suite. The shower was refreshing, his dental status appreciative of a once-around with a disposable hospital toothbrush. Ready for a night on the town, Jackson exited the restroom, anticipating some fun.

Patrice Summers brought her outfit to the hospital that morning in a backpack she stored in the surgery call room. She stood with expectation in the hallway, waiting for her date. Dressed for an exciting night in a black leather oversized shouldered jacket, she wore a pink knit miniskirt dress. Patrice wore gray-colored pantyhose, black high-heeled pumps, and carried a small pink clutch purse as an accessory. She puffed up and styled her brown hair perfectly, accentuating it with a streak. Dressed for the night, she waited for fun.

Jackson smiled at Patrice, putting his arm around her shoulder as the two made their way to the parking lot below. He dressed much like usual, wearing a long-sleeved, button-down, pale blue shirt, black corduroy pants, and his newly polished iguana skin cowboy boots. He threw his dark brown leather jacket over his shoulder, relieved to leave the hospital for the night.

Lee W. Hickok tuned his FM radio, looking for something they could enjoy. He was idling his 1972, metallic green Datsun 240Z in the doctor's parking lot looking for some fun. He wore a crisp brown sports jacket, pale blue shirt, navy-blue ironed slacks, and signature cream-colored snakeskin cowboy boots. A dutifully tied Windsor knotted brown and blue tie completed his attire. The radio played *Gonna Dance with Somebody* by Whitney Houston as Jackson politely opened the door for Patrice.

"We have reservations for eight o'clock at The Midtown Chophouse, Lee W. It is on Front Street in Palo Alto. Do you know the way?" Jackson was sitting in the rear hatch. Turning off his pager, he realized his hunger.

"Oh, I love Whitney. Lee W.. Can you turn it up?" Patrice wondered, swaying in her seat.

Lee W. turned the radio up loud. "I know the way. Welcome to your magic carpet ride, y'all."

•   •   •   •   •

The Chophouse was an old, established restaurant in downtown Palo Alto. It was famous for thick grilled steaks and fresh fish dishes. When Lee W. proposed a night out at that institution courtesy of him, Jackson wondered about its prices. A phone call, making their reservations, confirmed his suspicions. His attending was in for an expensive night.

"We have a reservation for Hickok at eight. It was for three and by the fireplace. Is that still okay?" Lee W. enquired.

"It will be about fifteen minutes, Dr. Hickok. Make yourselves comfortable. The bar is to your right."

Jackson looked at Lee W. with a knowing smile. He was now sober for one year from his narcotic addiction. Lee W. was as well, one year dry.

"Where is the restroom?"

"Through the bar on the left, Dr. Hickok."

•   •   •   •   •

"I will have. Well, let's see, y'all. Give me a club soda with a twist. Your drink is empty, my dear. Bring the lady another. What are you drinking?"

An attractive woman sat by herself on a leather seated barstool as Lee W. sat down. "An Old Fashion."

•　　•　　•　　•　　•

The announcement overhead said: "Hickok. Party of three."

"We will seat you now, Dr. Cooper."

Jackson looked around for Lee W. as the welcomer led them to their table. "Here are your menus. Enjoy your meal."

"Jackson, I hope Lee W. heard his name. You don't think?"

Jackson began looking at the priceless menu. He was concerned as well. He recalled Lee W.'s reference to his old sweet amber when they were alone in his office. The man asked him to add it to his coffee. But then he was joking? Wasn't he? "Here he comes."

Lee W. arrived, a clear liquid glass with a lemon twist in his hand. He was talking to a girl following him as he set the tumbler at his seat. He ushered the girl to the table. "Jackson. Patrice. This is Bunny."

The girl looked like an MTV diva, with a short blond fashionably spiked hairstyle, sparkling beautiful blue eyes, and perfectly applied, but thick, makeup. She wore a black silver studded short leather jacket and looked ready for the dance floor. She was perfect in her appearance, outfitted in olive green high-waisted high-cuffed pants, a beige silk blouse, and silver high-heeled shoes.

Lee W. held the chair out for Bunny as she sat and smiled at the two. "Hi, Patrice," she said, shaking her hand. Turning to Jackson, she asked. "What was your name?".

"Jackson, Bunny. Jackson Cooper."

"Bunny is from Florida. Isn't that right, Bunny?" Lee W. pulled out his chair and sat. He pointed to his drink and shook his head no with a deliberate smile.

"Yes, I am. Jacksonville."

An uncomfortable silence filled the table. Lee W. picked up his menu and said: "I am famished."

The waitress brought water. She recited the specials on the menu without, of course, mentioning their prices.

"What do you do, Jackson and Patrice?" Bunny smiled. She looked down at her menu. "The halibut is great here, I hear."

Jackson spoke for the two. "We are physicians at UMC, Bunny. Patrice is a plastic surgeon. I am an urologist, like Lee W." Jackson looked down at his menu. "I want a rib-eye. I am a carnivore."

"You are all doctors? How exciting."

"We are residents at the university. Lee W. is an attending. He is an assistant professor." Patrice was not looking at the menu. From the first moment, she fixed her gaze on the girl.

•   •   •   •   •

In the parking lot, the four stood talking. Bunny took Lee W.'s arm in hers. She bumped against the man and playfully grabbed a handful of his tie. "Lee W., let's go dancing. I know this wonderful spot. The Frosty Barrel. It's right down the street."

Jackson looked exhausted. Patrice was yawning. Lee W. was smiling. "My car is over here. Y'all up for this?" Lee W. moved to his car. He opened the back hatch with his key. On the passenger side, he opened the door and ushered Bunny to sit.

•   •   •   •   •

The Frosty Barrel was a loud, neon-lit, packed disco dancing joint. A line encircled the entire establishment's length. Loud blaring music thundered. A large man in black leather took cash and signaled the four to join the line. That is until he spied Bunny.

"Bunny." The man signaled to the girl. The two then laughed and talked. Soon he raised the rope, and the four moved into the Barrel.

A crowd filled the place, and it was dark inside. The air was icy, cloudy, and smelled of tobacco-laced perspiration. Loud disco music played overhead. Filled booths surrounded a large, raised, packed dance floor on the periphery. Twirling disco balls reflected lights across the room. Bunny led the group. There was one open booth, and the four piled in.

Bunny grabbed a waitress. She stood and yelled in the girl's ear. "Shirley, beers for everyone. Get me a Mai Tai. This place is great tonight." She slipped away to the girl's restroom.

When she returned, she sat down and downed her drink. "This place is happening. It's wild. I come here all the time." Bunny was laughing. She evidently was in her element. Donna Summers screamed through the PA system. "We work hard for the money..."

Bunny grabbed Lee W. and deposited him on the dance floor. The night and the music bumped along. Bunny danced with all. She was continually on the go. Lee W., Jackson, and Patrice were not immune to her advances. She was determined and refused to accept a no. The girl danced with other men. She danced with many women. The night grew late.

One time on the dance floor, Bunny stopped dancing. She pulled Lee W. to her and kissed him on the lips. Bunny startled Lee W. with her aggression. He licked his lips and put his finger to his mouth. "Are you high, Bunny?" The girl laughed at the man. Lee W. licked his lips again. He had tasted that taste before.

"I need to go pee, Lee W. My purse. It's in your car. Let me have your key." Bunny reached into Lee W.'s front pocket and quickly retrieved his car keys. She turned and left the floor.

When he returned to the booth, Jackson took him aside. "Lee W. Patrice and I are due in the hospital early in the morning. Could you take us home?"

In the parking lot, the three walked along in silence. Finally, Patrice said: "Where did you get that girl, Lee W. She was high. She is a hooker!"

"I tasted cocaine on her lips. Sorry gang. Won't happen again."

Patrice stopped suddenly. "The Datsun was parked right in that spot! Lee W., where did your car go? Oh, no. And where is Bunny?"

CHAPTER 10

Jackson Cooper watched the kitchen clock tick away. It was 10:05 p.m., and the resident was home, studying for the last hour. Tomorrow, he would wake at 5:00 a.m., and leave for the hospital at 5:15. Rounds were at 5:30, and the OR began at seven. Between now and waking up, he had 6 hours and 55 minutes.

Sleep was the elusive factor for Jackson. He felt thankful, for he was only on call every third night. On call then, he spent the 24-hour interval in the hospital. He stayed in the hospital until late on his two days off. After the third day, the call schedule would rewind.

He appreciated his intern, Mike Nelson, who came to him today and insisted that he leave the hospital at a decent hour to gain an ample night's sleep. Mike would cover for Jackson. The next day, he would perform the most important surgery of his life. Jackson was exhausted. He needed to catch up tonight. It was a meat grinder lifestyle that left you never fully acclimated. Sleep deprivation from the call schedule weighed heavily on the resident.

The stove timer rang as he sat at his small, round, white Formica-covered table in his studio apartment in Mountain View. Jackson stood, opened the range, and removed a steaming hot TV dinner. He peeled back the tinfoil covering. What stared back at him, chicken and dumplings, incensed the man. He was furious and pulled the old box from the trash.

Threatening under his breath, he read the cardboard container: *Swanson Corn Beef Hash Dinner*. He compared the photograph on the box to his meal. Now livid, he noted no resemblance. Swanson mislabeled his precious feast.

He grabbed the tray with a potholder and tossed it on the table. The clock now read 10:12, just 6 hours and 48 minutes until he had to wake. Jackson calmed himself. He sat at the table and picked up a surgical atlas. As he read, the resident blew air on the entrée and took a tentative bite.

It calmed Jackson when he remembered that tomorrow morning was the surgical event of his career. Dr. Elmer Crabb chose him to perform the anatrophic nephrolithotomy on Wei Huan over the chief resident Tara Patel. The latter would second assist that day, but Jackson was the primary surgeon.

The surgical atlas showcased illustrations and photos of the procedure's twenty steps. He had been memorizing these today. He closed his eyes, reviewed, and recreated each step.

The clock now said 10:22 p.m., another ten minutes gone. Jackson began eating his chicken and dumplings between bites, reading the atlas' text descriptions. When complete, he picked up a journal article Tara recommended on the procedure. 10:45 p.m., just six hours and 25 minutes until awake time. Anxiety was building.

The night wore on similarly. During his reading, he constantly checked the clock almost every minute. He perused the atlas, *Glenn's Urologic Surgery*, *Campbell's Textbook of Urology*, and several journal articles by Dr. Crabb and Dr. Bolton. He memorized pictures and text descriptions, closed his eyes, and visualized their contents. As the hours dwindled, he began to feel panic in the pit of his stomach. Would he have enough sleep before tomorrow's critical case? 11:22 p.m., just five hours and 28 minutes.

He adjourned to his bed. After a quick shower, he lay his head down, refreshed but wide awake. 11:47 p.m. now registered on his Mickey Mouse alarm clock. He set the silly clock's alarm for five a.m..

Then the dreaded restless leg syndrome began (RLS). RLS is an inherited condition where an electric-like twinge stabs periodically through the patient's leg. When tired, generally at night, this feeling would suddenly force the sufferer to move his leg. The ultimate result was when RLS was present. The sufferer can not sleep.

Jackson struggled with the RLS, tried to forget and go to sleep. As always, with RLS, he was unsuccessful. 12:27 p.m. now registered, and his fear of not sleeping before this big case grew. At 1:15 a.m., he gave up and got out of bed. He paced in his bedroom. Troubling thoughts of his past filtered into his exhausted brain.

About one year ago, he was dead in the urology call room at UMC. His Percocet addiction had progressed to using intravenous Fentanyl stolen from anesthesia in the operating room. Patrice found him with an empty IV syringe still in his vein. She resuscitated Jackson with an amp of the narcotic antagonist Narcan and performed CPR.

The images of his addiction began clouding his mind. Hoping to find a hiding place, he jumped into a cold shower. Longing for just a small dose of narcotic, he sat at the kitchen table. He remembered that he never failed to sleep while high on drugs. He grabbed the old Percocet bottle. Remnants of Percocet odor lingered in the container. TIC TACS failed to satisfy this time.

He moved to his bedroom closet, where he found a near-empty syringe and tourniquet wrapped in an old sock. A drop of liquid was present at the syringe's bottom.

Jackson sat at the kitchen table, clearing it of the TV tray and textbooks. The resident wrapped the tourniquet around his left arm. He thought. He cried, but he couldn't go through with it.

Laying in his bed, he felt some pride. About ready to triumph, he faced his demon. He quickly jumped and knelt by the bed for prayer. He wouldn't remember his words to the Lord, but it was enough.

When the alarm went off, Jackson realized he slept through the night. The RLS was gone, but more importantly, temporarily, at least, the evil tormentor of drugs was gone. Wei Huan was on the schedule, and Jackson Cooper was on his way.

•　　　•　　　•　　　•　　　•

Jackson Cooper was in the surgeon's lounge. He was very nervous, this case was the biggest of his life. He pulled down a urologic surgery atlas and sat on the old, worn couch to review.

An anatrophic nephrolithotomy was an operation where the surgeons removed a large staghorn stone from the kidney. After making a large incision, they exposed the kidney. The surgeons then incised the kidney meat radially between the arteries, and they peeled open the organ like two clam halves. This maneuver allowed the removal of the large centralized stone. They left a large nephrostomy tube for urinary drainage. After surgery, a sterile magnesium salt solution called Renacidin circulated through this tube. Renacidin then dissolved any residual stone fragments left behind. The surgery would last four hours if successful.

•　　　•　　　•　　　•　　　•

They dropped the temperature in the OR suite for the big cases. Jackson entered room two with a yellow coverup wrapped around him over his green scrub suit. He moved to the phone on the wall and called the intern. "Mike, bring Mr. Huan's x-ray boat to room two. Make sure the CAT scan and IVP are in the jacket."

Jackson could not be more excited. He felt rested after his complicated night. He moved to the head of the operating table. Anesthesia was busy laying out their drugs and instruments. "Hi, Andre." Andre was a big Samoan man dressed in a huge green scrub suit, a too-small stretchy blue surgery hat, and a tight-fitting mask. He trained at the University of Samoa, finishing an unlikely fellowship in pediatric anesthesiology at UCLA. A big, sweet man, he was quite capable. Jackson felt comfortable with the anesthesia team.

Nurse Kelley was the scrub nurse today. She would stand with the surgeons, hand and collect instruments, sutures, sponges, and clips. Kelley was busy in sterile gloves and gown, opening instrument trays and stacking the massive number of shiny stainless-steel instruments on the back table. Checking the instruments, she made sure none remained in the wound. Martha was the circulating nurse. Her job was to move around the room, distribute supplies, and help the scrub nurse and surgeons. Quiet music played overhead as she wiped down the black operating table and moved the large overhead lights into place.

Mike was at the door with the x-ray boat. "They are all in here, Jackson. Tara is coming. I haven't seen EJC yet. I'll be in and out today. Got so much to do."

Jackson took the x-ray jacket, pulled the films, and snapped them on the view box. The large staghorn stone remained unchanged from before, as shown by the KUB. The CAT scan revealed the kidney, artery, and vein size, and shape. The IVP, or intravenous pyelogram, was an x-ray after intravenous dye. The kidneys picked up the dye, and a picture of the inside or collecting system containing the staghorn resulted.

A gurney pushed the door open, and Mr. Huan rolled in. Wei entered the operating room on a gurney, feeling the chilly air. At the table, the transportation staff and Nurse Martha transferred the man onto the operating table. Wei used his arms to transfer himself onto the operating table. Overhead lights illuminated the room, while a quiet buzzing emanated from the staff. They laid him back, placed a mask on his face, and inserted an IV into his neck.

Jackson moved to his side. He nodded a confident yes and rubbed the man's chest affectionately. He pulled up his gown and marked the intended incision over Wei's left flank with a sterile purple pen.

Tara and EJC entered next. She would stand at the bottom of the table, the second assistant, helping Jackson on the patient's left. Tara nodded to Jackson and moved to view the x-rays. EJC would assist on the right. The professor wore a vintage white crumpled scrub suit and a red and black floral cotton hat tied in the back. As was his practice, he did not wear a mask. Something about airflow and his pre-war training convinced the professor that it was excessive and unnecessary.

"Mr. Huan, I will pre-oxygenate you with this anesthesia mask. Just breathe normally." Andre was ready to begin and coached the patient with soft words. A large IV was already in the patient's neck, and he slipped some Fentanyl into the tubing. "You will feel a warm rush in your neck and face; then you won't be aware. Nighty Night, Mr. Huan."

"You'll be all right, Mr. Huan." Jackson Cooper appeared at his side, his face obscured by a mask. The resident briefly grabbed the patient's hand. Drugs quickly affected Wei, making the room swim as he fell asleep.

The patient was quickly asleep, and Andre moved swiftly to establish an airway. He pulled his head and neck back into extension and slipped a large, clear plastic endotracheal tube through his mouth and into his trachea. He then taped the tube to the side of Wei's face.

Martha moved to the abdomen. She removed Wei's hospital gown and began scrubbing with sponges and iodine-containing soap. The team went to the scrub sinks to wash.

The surgeons crowded around the operating table after being gowned by Kelley. They adjusted the overhead lights, and Jackson asked for a scalpel.

Jackson made a large incision on the marked skin. Using an electro-cautery bovie, he began the dissection. Jackson wondered about EJC's feelings about bovies. On one of his visits to the professor's office, he asked about their use. He remembered his response exactly as he dissected along. "If it is good enough for William T. Bovie on October 1, 1926, at Peter Bent Brigham, it is good enough for you reprobates. I may be old, but don't underestimate my contemporary usage of technology, Dr. Cooper."

Today's procedure was the fourth stone surgery performed on this patient. As expected, scar and edematous tissue encased the abdomen and kidney. Slowly, after about an hour, they exposed the kidney.

EJC was holding a steel sucker canula and pointing out various structures. "Tell us your plan, Dr. Cooper. Brief and to the point."

"Well, after exposing the kidney, we need to dissect free the main renal artery and vein." Renal was a term for kidney, a much more clinical term. "We need to get silastic tape around them. Then clamp the vessels."

"In what order?"

"First, the artery, allowing the blood in the kidney to escape through the vein. Then clamp the vein." Jackson was ready for the man. Performing these maneuvers in the reverse order allowed the kidney to expand and often explode. Quite a catastrophe he planned to bypass.

They accomplished the vascular maneuvers, and the blood flow to the kidney quenched. "Where will you incise the parenchyma of the kidney, Dr. Cooper?" Here the question involved splitting the kidney radially like a clam.

"There is an avascular plane of Brodel, Dr. Crabb. To reduce bleeding, we use that plane to incise the kidney between the small arteries and veins."

Jackson performed this maneuver smoothly and with relative ease. With the kidney now split open, they visualized the large staghorn stone. With hemostats and forceps, they broke the stone up and removed it piecemeal. A tube remained in the kidney, emerging through the skin as a nephrostomy tube. This tube was for urine drainage, as well as irrigation postoperatively.

They began closing when Andre stopped them. "Give me a moment, Jackson. I don't like his cardiac rhythm."

Jackson and Tara stepped away from the operating table. A rapid tracing appeared on the man's EKG.

"V-Tach, people. I am infusing lidocaine now." Andre was concerned with a rapid, abnormal cardiac rhythm. Wei's blood pressure was low. The lidocaine did nothing. "I am giving him 150 mg of Amiodarone." With the second anti-arrhythmic, Amiodarone, the heart slowed and began a normal sinus rhythm. Wei's blood pressure stabilized. Everyone could breathe again. "Okay, people. Can you finish up, Jackson?"

In the recovery room, Jackson viewed the patient. He examined his dressing, nephrostomy tube, and urinary output. He was especially aware of his EKG tracing, which continued in normal sinus rhythm. Mike arrived, carrying the x-ray boat under his arm. "I promised them I would return these films to radiology. How did Wei do?"

Jackson moved to the nursing station. He plopped down in a chair, took off his surgical hat, and tossed it in the trash container. He considered removing his cowboy boots but thought he would wait for the surgeon's lounge. "It went relatively well, Mike. Keep in mind, however, that he had a run of V-Tach. They used Amiodarone. Anesthesia wants him on a drip post-op. Give him Amiodarone 1000 mg IV over 24 hours. How much is that per hour?"

Mike was a wiz with numbers. He thought and answered: "That is about 42 mg per hour. I will order it, Jackson. Can we visit the family together?"

"Family, I wasn't aware of any. Are they in the OR waiting room?"

Mike moved to the nursing station. The clerk, Kathy, was busy stamping papers for Wei's chart. "Kathy, where is the family?"

"In the waiting room. But I believe it is just one person, Dr. Nelson."

Wei woke in the surgical intensive care unit with a tube in his lungs, IV poles and tubing hooked to his neck and arms, and a nephrostomy tube flowing with urine. The man had previous surgical experiences. His hemicorpectomy was in 1961. Similar stone surgeries followed in 1968, '71, and '78. He was an old pro. However, he was tired of it.

He was asleep and still on the ventilator when Maury stood beside him.

"Hi Wei, I can only stay until the nurse kicks me out. They say the surgery went well. No more stones, my friend."

Wei wrote out a question on a clipboard for Maury. It read: *Where is the little man?*

"Who is the little man, Wei? Oh, you mean Dr. Crabb."

Wei shook his head yes.

"Maurice, you need to leave now." The nurse entered the room. She touched Maurice on his shoulder and led him out. He looked back over his shoulder, waved, and said goodbye to Wei.

•　　　•　　　•　　　•　　　•

A petite Asian girl was sitting in the waiting room alone. She seemed to read a book and watch the news on the overhead television simultaneously.

"Are you here for Mr. Huan?" Jackson and Mike entered the surgery waiting room and stood before the girl.

She stood politely, nodded quietly, and silently smiled at the two surgeons. She was just a head taller than the level of Jackson's belt. She had kind, solid black eyes and beautiful straight black hair cut in a pageboy fashion. She wore a floral high-waisted dress and red flat-heeled shoes. "Dr.'s, how is my uncle?"

Jackson was curious. "How old are you?"

"Twelve. Twelve and a half, actually." As she spoke, she smiled, her bright eyes wide with enthusiastic confidence.

"How did you get here?" She was alone, of course, too young to drive.

"The bus. I got here at eight this morning." She put out her arm and shook the two men's hands. "My name is Li. Glad to meet you. Are you Dr. Cooper?"

Jackson felt embarrassed. He was so surprised by her maturity and young age he had not answered her question. "Li, this is Dr. Nelson. Yes, I am Dr. Cooper. He's fine. Your uncle is fine. Wei did very well."

Li smiled a big, beautiful smile. She turned and picked up her book from the couch. Now Jackson realized it was a King James Bible. Turning to the back page, she produced a small pink flower. "This is for you, Dr. Cooper. I don't have one for Dr. Nelson. So sorry."

The girl was a burst of fresh air. She spent several days around the hospital, always smiling and respectful. Wei was so proud and happy to see her.

CHAPTER 11

"Stella, call a code. He is having a seizure!" Wei Huan was having a grand-mal seizure, jerking with violent muscular contractions involving his entire body. Stella jumped and raised the head of the bed, maintaining the man's airway by extending his head and neck. She followed her teaching and elected not to place anything into his mouth. As her instructor said, no one can swallow their tongue. Wei continued to seize with forced exhalation and chest contraction, creating a moaning cry. He expelled foamy saliva from his mouth under pressure, which coated his lips.

Before the seizure, Wei expressed the feeling of impending doom with the smell of a burnt aroma and nausea just minutes before. He then lost consciousness, his eyes rolled back, and the seizure activity began.

Mike Nelson was hurrying down the hallway when he heard the code. Nurses and staff followed him into the room, bringing carts of drugs and an EKG machine. Mike drew up 10 mg of Valium in a syringe, moved to the bedside, and pushed the drug through Wei's IV. He reached the nephrostomy tube's Renacidin, turning the drip off. They ran an EKG, supplied oxygen through a mask, and gradually the seizure subsided.

Jackson Cooper was leaving the operating room when he heard the call from the urology floor overhead. He rushed to the elevators and arrived, out of breath, in Mr. Huan's room. The atmosphere calmed. The patient's tonic-clonic seizure activity was now gone. He was unconscious, in a post-ictal state, that condition after a grand mal seizure. Wei inhaled rhythmically, deep with a loud exhalation, spewing a salvo of saliva with each breath.

Mike looked at the EKG tracing. Valium quickly solved the problem. He was grateful, but what caused the patient's seizure? The tracing showed a rapid heart rate, as expected during a seizure, but was otherwise unchanged. Morning labs were pending, but the patient was well otherwise.

Jackson looked the patient over. His shortened body again touched him. His wound was healing well. The resident found clear breath sounds, and his abdomen soft with normal bowel sounds. Jackson noted nothing of note on his physical, except that his skin was quite flushed. The drip of Renacidin stood out to the resident. Could this drug be responsible?

Renacidin was a salt-containing solution used for years to dissolve kidney stones. Here, its purpose was to dissolve any residual, even microscopic, stone fragments not removed at surgery. It dripped from a clear liquid bag above the bedside, infusing through the nephrostomy tube.

Jackson read the label on the Renacidin. It comprised citric acid, gluconic delta-lactne, and magnesium carbonate. The resident was unfamiliar with the chemistry or the drugs' properties. "Mike, draw some red stoppered tubes for labs. Run a stat magnesium level. See if the lab can measure citrate levels. Let's not restart the Renacidin."

Jackson hurried to the urology library. He soon came across an obscure report of seizures during Renacidin kidney irrigations. Here, the medical team noted several patients had high blood magnesium levels. They proposed measuring these levels serially around the clock. The study treated levels above 2.5 milligrams per deciliter with immediate Renacidin discontinuation. In addition, the Swedish paper suggested a water manometer on the irrigation tubing. They believed it was mandatory to maintain a pressure of under 20 centimeters of water pressure.

Jackson walked across the hallway to the urology department's office. Here, four secretaries were busy typing, writing, and making phone calls. "Rebecca, can I use your phone to call the lab?"

Jackson arrived at the W3B nursing station with a handwritten list of Mr. Huan's morning and stat labs. He was carrying a package with a plastic water manometer. Mike sat writing progress notes. The resident handed him the list, which he skimmed. "What is this, Jackson?"

"I got his labs. They are from the morning draw and the ones you got after Wei's seizure. Mike, his magnesium is 6.0!" Jackson handed a box to the intern. "This is what he requires for his nephrostomy tube." He found a clear plastic tube with centimeter markings from zero to 40. At the bottom was a red plastic stopcock, which allowed plugging into the nephrostomy tubing.

The two moved to Wei's bedside. Stella and nurse Keri were cleaning him up. The man lay still, his eyes open but glazed. He was breathing normally now and smiled a small smile in recognition. "Mr. Huan. You look back from the dead."

"The manometer must be at the kidney's height, Mike. Plug it in." Jackson handed the nephrostomy tubing to the intern, who coupled the manometer into the system. Soon the drip was running, but the fluid column in the clear plastic device registered 38 centimeters of water pressure. Jackson turned off the drip. He looked at the intern. "That pressure is way too high. That's probably why he seized."

Jackson had an idea. He broke the column off at 20 centimeters and restarted the drip. Soon the device was running, but the liquid spilled over the top and onto the floor. Jackson then lowered the bag, and the spillage stopped. That the device now only allowed 20 centimeters of pressure was a fail-safe mechanism.

At the nursing station, Jackson handed Mike the chart on Mr. Huan. "Write for stat, q six, serum magnesiums, Mike." The order would instruct the blood drawers to draw a serum magnesium level every six hours around the clock. "The person on call needs to follow this level. Stop the Renacidin if it is above 2.5, without fail. Show Stella and Keri how to adjust the pressure."

There were no more seizures on W3B.

•   •   •   •   •

The sign announced that:

FINALLY, UMC presents the return of *DUCK SOUP! Served now, Wednesday through Saturday.*

For years, Jackson Cooper stood looking at the white-lettered, brown corkboard-fashioned sign hanging at the UMC main cafeteria entrance. His exhausted physician's brain had a comedic flash. Rearranging the letters to read FUCK soup would be hilarious. His quiet personality said no to this.

Duck soup was the resident's favorite. It was a meaty broth with floating chunks of mystery meat, reportedly duck. It looked and smelled horrible but was quite delicious. Jackson missed its presence on the menu. He would have to get himself a large bowl.

There was just a small line waiting for the cafeteria's suspect cuisine. Jackson stood anxiously waiting for the cook, Cookie, to dish him a bowl of Duck soup. He went to the check-out line with his portion on a brown plastic tray. It was a call night. By protocol, he could sign for all that he could eat. He stopped and grabbed four pieces of sourdough with three slices of chocolate cream pie. He would store the extra for later in the call room.

"You eat Duck soup, Jackson?"

Jackson turned to his tall friend, James Marks, an internist who attended the same medical school in Boston. "I call it FUCK soup, Jim. It is great, though; I am glad it is back."

"I don't eat what I can't identify. You got enough pie? Turns your blood to mayonnaise, Jackson."

"My blood's already mayonnaise."

"Say, I am taking care of Barbara Jennings. Ring a bell? You know, Barbara *Bunny* Jennings. She is in the ICU. She wrote a friendly note asking for you."

Jackson turned in surprise. He must have flashed his teeth with anger or something. Jim stepped back, saying: "Wow! Quite a memory, I guess, Jackson. She's a hooker, you know. Stage four HIV/AIDS. She is dying of pneumocystis. You ought to come see her. Don't bother with flowers."

Jackson entered the Medical ICU nursing station. He grabbed Bunny's chart, sat, and read. It turns out that she had known her HIV status for about a year, months before their fateful meeting. She presented last week with full-blown AIDS. Bunny quickly developed respiratory failure requiring emergent intubation and ventilator support in the ICU. She had the usual Pneumocystis jirovecii pneumonia or PCP. This is an opportunistic fungal infection of the lungs seen almost entirely in immunocompromised patients with AIDS.

Except for the ventilator, the room was quiet and strangely ice-cold. Bunny lay on her back, an endotracheal ventilator tube exiting her mouth, secured to her mottled checks with strips of white paper tape. She looked 20 pounds lighter, covered only with a single white sheet. They taped her eyes shut, and her hair was patchy and now gray. A large purplish Kaposi's sarcoma nearly consumed her nose. Jackson was mad at her. He recalled her appearance at the Chophouse, her wicked seduction of Lee W., her dancing, and her theft of his sports-car. The resident recalled walking to the bus station with Patrice and Lee W. that night. It was late. They could not even grab a cab.

Jackson calmed himself. Anger and resentment were not in his nature. They were emotions that did not seem appropriate anymore.

CHAPTER 12

Maurice Latinsky's spiking fevers disappeared after the ureteral exploration and TB abscess drainage by Dr Patel and Hickok. Before this procedure, he had nightly 103-degree fevers with shaking chills. Now, through the night, his vital signs were normal.

While the patient improved clinically, his underlying immunocompromised status continued and slowly progressed. Measuring T Cell lymphocyte counts was the accepted process of measuring the immune system's effectiveness in HIV/AIDS patients. A normal T-Cell count called a CD4 count, for people with healthy immune systems is 500 to 1500 cells per cubic millimeter of blood. HIV patients have levels below 500. AIDS begins with counts below 200. On admission, now several months ago, Maurice had a count of 174. His value now hovered in the 75 range. It was a matter of time before this allowed him to contract an AIDS-related disease such as pneumocystis pneumonia, toxoplasmosis, or Kaposi's sarcoma.

The UMC urology team felt Maurice suffered from HIV-related dementia. He had lapses in consciousness, difficulty with thinking, and memory lapses. In addition, he continued to experience deeply disturbing delusions and hallucinations. His Steve McQueen fantasy certainly was still present and active. His obsession with escaping the confines of the hospital continued.

Frederick Bishop, known as Freddie, arrived that morning with fresh flowers for Maurice and a secret gift. He wore a pink and white pinstriped suit, a red silk shirt, a matching pinstripe pink bowtie, and shiny penny loafer shoes. A red carnation on his lapel completed his outfit.

"It is dark and so stuffy in here, my dear." Freddie opened the curtains of Maurice's room and turned on some lights. He tossed the old and put the new red and pink carnations in a vase on the nightstand. The man carried a brightly wrapped box tied with a cheerful red ribbon. He ceremoniously presented the gift to Maurice. Quietly, he picked up Maurice's partially filed urinal and dumped the contents into the toilet. Freddie then sat down on the bed and clapped quietly.

"What's this, Freddie?" Maurice had just awakened in the morning. He remained in bed, covered with a down comforter that Freddie had brought previously.

Freddie raised the head of the bed with the bedside control. He then helped Maurice to sit up. There was confusion on the patient's face as he unsuccessfully tried to open his gift. "Let me help you, dear. See. The wrapping comes off, and then just open the top of the box, Maury."

Freddie helped complete the unwrapping. He lifted the gift from its box and set it on the nightstand. A vintage drab green, metal German helmet complete with an emblem of a folded down wings eagle clutching a swastika in its talons appeared. He took the helmet and carefully put it on Maurice's head.

•　　•　　•　　•　　•

The night was a rough one for Maurice Latinsky. While he suffered no further high fevers, nightly dreams of riding away on dirt-laden roads in Nazi-occupied Europe on the usual motorbike often tormented him. He awoke at 5:00 a.m., afraid to return to sleep.

He dressed quickly, avoiding the soon-to-be nursing visit. Standing before his bedside mirror, he admired himself. He wore hospital-issued jammies, his brown cardigan sweater, and a thin terrycloth robe with white slippers. With ceremony, he took the helmet and set it on his head. He wondered if he could make it. The urinal with urine loomed in his mind. He picked it up, rejected the thought, and put it back down. Turning now to his journey, he believed he was ready.

The ward was silent when Maurice entered the darkened hallway of W3B. He padded along, no one in sight. At room one, he silently opened the room door and slipped inside.

Wei Huan lay in his bed snoring. The medical staff attached IVs to Wei Huan and drained and irrigated his left nephrostomy tube with the Renacidin solution.

"Wei, are you awake?"

Wei Huan slowly opened his eyes, feeling overwhelmed with joy, while his now dear friend stared at him closely. A curious metal helmet sat on Maurice's head.

"Wei, they are after me."

"Who, Maury?"

"The goons, you know the Krauts, they will be here any moment. They will lock me up in the cooler for sure. You got to let me hide here, Wei."

"Maury, are you sure? Only nurses are here. You are safe; shouldn't you be sleeping?" Wei pulled himself up and sat on the bed. He, too, had been having bad dreams. His friend concerned him, however. He was aware of Maury's delusional fantasy. "Where did you get that German helmet, Maury?"

Maury's thoughts cleared. He realized where he was. Suddenly he remembered the helmet was Freddie's gift, not of military issue. He looked down at his clothing. The brown cardigan sweater was a gift from Freddie as well. He realized he had been dreaming. Maury started sobbing.

Wei pushed the nursing call button.

•   •   •   •   •

Cam Thompson chose to end his life with a shotgun blast to his head. While his life was spared, his aim was faulty. The result was a devastating injury to his face. He was just beginning to process what he had done to himself.

Exhausted, Patrice made her way to the ICU. Cam was due again for a facial dressing change. She mastered the around-the-clock procedures, getting supplies and a syringe of morphine from the pharmacist.

"How are you tonight, Cam?" After she said that, she was sorry. It was a throwaway question at best, and Patrice realized how insincere it must have sounded. The man was a tragic disaster. The blast ripped away his lower jaw and most of his face, leaving behind an open wound of raw, bleeding flesh. His right eye was gone, the left eye intact, signaling and receiving messages from a tormented brain. Cam looked at Patrice; he blinked repeatedly and tried to calm down.

Patrice laid her supplies on the over-bed tray. She took the morphine, stuck the needle into the IV port, and pushed 2 mg of pain-relieving medication as a pre-med for what she was about to do. Suddenly, Cam reached for the syringe with overpowering strength. He dislodged Patrice's hand for just a moment and tried to empty the entire syringe into his IV.

"Oh no. No. No. Cam!" Patrice wrestled the syringe out of Cam's hand. She took the medication, recapped the needle, and placed it out of reach on the nightstand. She was out of breath but looked closely in the patient's eye. Fear, dread, and an element of self-hatred flashed back. The resident took her clipboard and placed a pen in Cam's hand. "It's for your pain when we change your dressings, Cam. That syringe is full of morphine. Don't do that. I get it, everything will be fine."

NO, IT WON'T. Cam scribbled across the paper. Tears came to his eye.

"It is tough. But, please, you got to go on." Patrice was not sure inside. The man faced a long, tortuous course. His life would never be the same. The problems that caused his suicide attempt were only going to get worse. Much worse.

Patrice never contemplated suicide. She struggled to comprehend those who did. They must experience intolerable mental anguish and anticipation that it will never disappear. Her life was challenging and demanding. She was mentally burnt and exhausted. But she never reached that point. What could she say to him? Patrice turned back to her task.

"I am going to give you another 2 mg, Cam. Don't you dare take the syringe again!"

As Patrice began the dressing changes, she thought about Jackson Cooper. She had to resuscitate him after a Fentanyl overdose in the surgery call room just over one year ago. Indeed, his addiction was out of control at that point. Was that a suicide attempt? She had never asked him. Then there was Lee W. Hickok. His alcoholism was legendary. No one intervened until he slit his wrist in a bathtub.

Patrice's answer was a simple one. She believed that Jesus Christ was her Lord and Savior. She believed that this fact saved her. All she knew was this truth, and she forced herself to tell Cam.

As she finished the dressing change, Patrice witnessed to the man. "Cam, I know you are distressed. It is overwhelming for you. I'm unsure of what to say. But Jesus is Lord. If you believe that you are saved. You can have eternal life. All this doesn't matter, Cam. "

Patrice could see the response in his blinking eye. A combination of self-commendation and relief. He raised the clipboard and wrote: **HOW TO BE SAVED?**

"Do you believe that Jesus Christ is the Son of God?"

YES, the boy wrote.

"Do you believe, Cam, that he who believes will have eternal life?"

Cam was crying now. Tears of joy ran down the remainder of his face. He scribbled: **YES**.

In the sterile supply room, Patrice wiped her face free of tears with a piece of gauze. She couldn't keep from crying. She was joyful, but apprehensive as well. Life is not as simple without salvation through Jesus Christ, believed the resident. Patrice pulled up a stool and sat alone.

Profound weariness crept over the physician. Patrice had been in the hospital for nearly 40 hours. Thirty minutes of interrupted sleep yesterday in the call room was her only respite. She witnessed clinical tragedies but overwhelming miracles in this noble profession called medicine. Perhaps Cam Jackson was now one of those.

CHAPTER 13

It was 8:30 on a Saturday night in Mountain View in September 1983. The Safeway parking lot was nearly empty as Jackson pulled in and parked his VW Bug. Patrice followed in her yellow Toyota Tercel, parking several cars away. They met at the store doors, grabbed a shopping basket, and entered.

The two residents tonight were surprised and appreciative of their time spent together. Unfortunately, Patrice was due back in the hospital in one hour. Jackson was off until tomorrow morning. Shopping wasn't a priority for house staff. They both had nothing to eat in their kitchens. They planned to catch up before their clinical assignments.

Jackson pushed the cart down the aisle. Silly piped-in music played overhead as they moved along. Despite his fatigue, he had to use his time to acquire food for the following week. He planned to sleep for twelve hours after returning to his apartment. He was excited and looking forward to the rest. Patrice did the shopping, grabbed an item, and tossed it into Jackson's cart. Patrice reported. "I need cereal, some sugar and coffee, and toilet paper. Don't let me forget the TP, Jackson. I am critical on that."

Jackson indicated he needed an ample supply of TV dinners, bread, milk, and eggs. "Swanson packaged a dinner in the wrong box the other day. I simply got furious because Swanson packaged a dinner in the wrong box, Patrice. The package said Swanson Corn Beef Hash, but I ended up with chicken and dumplings."

A thirty-ish male strolled past them, whistling to the overhead, so-called music. He wore a Kahiki long-sleeved shirt and pants, walked in black lace-up Doc Marten boots, and pushed a nearly full shopping cart. A Navy-blue USS Pasadena ball cap with gold piping sat on his head. Patrice smiled as he walked by.

Suddenly, the man's shopping cart turned over with a crash. Groceries tumbled out and across the floor. A carton of eggs lay open and crushed. He fell, pulling the pushcart. The man lay on his face. His body twisted below him. He had a bloody nose, and he was snoring loudly.

"Jackson! What the heck?" Patrice and Jackson rushed to the man. Kneeling now at his side, they felt his pulse and chest for breathing. "Jackson, he is asleep."

Jackson noted a medical alert bracelet on the man's arm. He read it carefully. "Says here that he has Narcolepsy, Patrice. His name is Terry H. Malone. His address is the Palo Alto VA hospital."

Narcolepsy is a sleep disorder that makes people very drowsy during the day. People with narcolepsy find it hard to stay awake for long periods of time. They fall asleep suddenly. This may cause severe problems in their daily routine.

"Mr. Malone, are you alright?" People were gathering around them. A store employee asked Patrice if they needed an ambulance. "Probably not now. Sir, wake up. Jackson, his pulse is strong, and he is breathing adequately. I think he just dropped off to sleep."

Jackson shook the man gently. He woke and sat on the floor with his back to the aisle. He was so sleepy looking, with a blank stare on his face, dried blood on his nose, some drool on the corner of his mouth. "I am okay. Just let me sit here for a while."

"Are you at the VA hospital, Mr. Malone?"

"A resident. I live there." The concept of people living in a hospital for extended lengths of time was new to the two residents. In reality, there were whole wards of chronically housed residents at the VA hospital next to the UMC.

Jackson recalled going to the VA for a urology consult. A man named Thomas Victor had blood in his urine. Jackson pulled and reviewed his chart. The hand written summary note read: Mr. Victor is a 64-year-old white man admitted to the hospital in December 1962. This was 1983. The reason for his admission was not apparent.

"What happened to you?" The man was waking up. He took out a handkerchief and wiped his nose of blood.

"I just fell asleep again. Happens to me all the time." Mr. Malone looked around at the crowd of people. Some anger flashed on his face. It must be frustrating, the condition so unpredictable and disruptive. "I will be okay. I'm going to sit here for a minute. It started in Vietnam in '72, after a helicopter crash. I have a head injury. Titanium. I am okay. Thanks for your help."

Reluctantly, Jackson and Patrice returned to their shopping.

•   •   •   •   •

Within a minute of her hospital arrival, her pager went off. The number was the ER. Patrice had an ominous, lousy feeling about it.

He was an African American named Buzzy. He evidently tried to take back a competitor's girlfriend who disagreed with the idea. The result, a gunshot wound to the abdomen from a 357-Magnum.

Buzzy was soon trying to die in the busy emergency department. The room was awash with personnel and piercing excitement. His feet were in the air in the Trendelenburg position. IVs were running full blast, blood was hanging, and the surgeons were crawling all over him. The goal was to stabilize the man and finish his nightmare in the operating room.

"James, what can I do?" Patrice wondered. James Tyrone was Surgery A's chief resident. He told Patrice last week that the next abdominal case was hers. Tonight, he kept his promise.

"Patrice, his BP is stabilizing with blood. We will get him to the OR. You can help me do the case."

•   •   •   •   •

The bullet entered the left upper quadrant of the abdomen. This region was spleen country. The stomach and left colon also lived there. Patrice made a large midline incision and explored the abdomen. The blast destroyed the spleen and left a huge hole in the colon.

James took Patrice through the removal of the spleen, a splenectomy. They resected the left colon, leaving a colostomy to divert the stool from the remaining colon and rectum. They vigorously irrigated the abdomen with liters of sterile water to wash out spilled bacteria. The man lost and received four units of blood. Patrice was tired, but faced a long night of babysitting Buzzy in the ICU.

In the recovery room, Patrice wrote orders, a post-operative note, dictated the operative procedure note, and then checked on Buzzy. The ward clerk informed her of the family's presence in the waiting room.

•   •   •   •   •

Patrice arrived in a crowded, small, dark room. As she stood at the door, two men hurriedly approached her. Hector was a small, brightly dressed man in a jogging outfit with a gold front tooth and a neon orange skull cap. He took a moment to obviously examine the doctor with his eyes. A smile came over him, and he winked several times with his right eye. His compadre, whose name was evidently Tooty, stood towering over him. Various individuals, including those with young ones, sat in the room. One woman sat by herself in the corner, crying quietly.

"I am Dr. Summers. Hector, Tooty, glad to meet you." Patrice shook the two men's hands. "Buzzy is all right. He is in the recovery room. We plan to keep him in the surgical ICU at least overnight. He lost a lot of blood. We had to remove his spleen and do a colostomy."

Hector continued to look Patrice over. He appeared as a carnivore, his constitution one of hunger. He wore a narrow smile on his face, and he constantly licked his gold tooth with his tongue. "You mean he has a shit bag?" Hector seemed happy. "Oh, he ain't gonna like that. No, he ain't, doc."

"It was necessary to save his life. When he reaches the ICU, one or two of you can see him."

"Tyesha, come meet Dr. Summers." Hector looked at Patrice's nametag on her white coat. "Patrice, that is a purrty name, doc. Tyesha, come talk to Patrice."

The woman in the corner stood and wiped away her tears with a tissue. In her early 20s, she was a tall, thin girl. She had a long wild afro hairstyle, bulging black eyes, long manicured nails, and a giant, tattooed snake winding across her neck. She tentatively strolled in high-heeled clogs to the door.

"Tyesha, glad to meet you. I am Dr. Summers." Patrice reached to Tyesha's hand and squeezed it.

"Tyesha, say hi to Patrice." Hector seemed angry with the girl. "Patrice here says Buzzy has a shit bag."

Tyesha looked down at the floor. She cried again. "I told him no biggie. No sir, no cat." Tyesha walked out, leaving her tissue behind.

Patrice buttoned up her coat. She nodded, turned, and slowly departed toward the ICU. She was tired. A long night of babysitting Buzzy in the ICU awaiting.

•   •   •   •   •

The night wore on. Buzzy was relatively stable. Patrice checked on the patient repeatedly. When satisfied, she considered moving to the call room for a nap. Something about the patient cautioned her. The bedside lay-back lounge chair loomed as a possibility. She pushed it directly over to the bedside. She took a warmed blanket, the edge spilling over the chair and onto the floor right up to the patient's bed. Patrice lay down, pulling the edge of the blanket over herself and falling asleep.

The ventilator puffed away rhythmically, Buzzy's chest repeatedly rising in response. His eyes were closed tightly, a nasogastric stomach tube in his nose. Hooked to suction, a low continuous whine whistled. Large-bore IVs exited his neck and arms. A large, sterile dressing covered his abdomen. Suction drains exited the wound. An empty colostomy bag lay over his upper right abdomen. Bladder catheter tubing drained yellow urine into a bag hooked to the side of the bed. Compression boots encircled his legs, whooshing with the same rhythm.

Tooty entered the room with stealth. He looked at the physician, now asleep, and laughed silently. The man moved to the bedside, standing on the edge of Patrice's blanket, staring at Buzzy.

Tooty was standing at the patient's side and smiling when Buzzy's eyes popped open with fright. The patient was frantic, shaking his head and moving his restrained arms at his side. "You be shamed, you piece of smeg." The invader pulled a black revolver with a long silencer from his shirt. He placed the muzzle against Buzzy's temple. "Bye, bye mafuka."

Tooty fell, face down, gun flying. A quick tug of the blanket dislodged and violently tumbled him to the floor. Patrice, like a cat, leaped from the chair onto the man. A violent struggle ensued. "Code. Code. Tucker, call a code."

The nurse quickly entered the room. He, too, jumped on Tooty. *Code Blue Surgical ICU* echoed overhead. Soon the room was full of the usual personnel. Security arrived promptly. They grabbed Tooty by his boots and forcefully dragged him out of the room, kicking and screaming.

Jackson arrived at the hospital that morning just when *Code Blue Surgical* ICU echoed overhead. He had a bad feeling as he ran to the escalators. He was passing the ICU waiting room when he heard his name.

"Jackson." Patrice stood at the door, her long brown hair tousled, her white coat dislodged and torn. Her red stethoscope hung from her pocket. She had on one rubber clog with a shoe cover, her other foot covered with only a white sock. Patrice took a deep breath and sighed a long sigh. She moved to the man and hugged him. "Where you been, Jackson?"

CHAPTER 14

Julie Mc Sweeney sat in the urology clinic again, looking pensive. She was a wary young woman, sporting a head of unruly red hair and a round, disgruntled face. She wore thick pancake makeup and bright red lipstick. Julie was short and portly, and her lack of height was obscured by her wearing high-heeled platform sandals. As she waited, as was her practice, she stood and inspected the cabinets and countertop supplies with her thick, stubby fingers. Her ever-present purse was full of hospital goods when she heard a quiet knock. As the door swung open, Julie quickly sat on the exam table.

"Hi, Ms. Mc Sweeney? How are you today? It's Dr. Cooper again."

"Terrible. Just terrible. My bladder feels like a jalapeno. I can't seem to pass up a single fricking toilet. You got to do something. Oh, and how are you? I love your tie. Is that a Bulgari?"

Jackson looked down at the patient's chart. His tie was from Target. "Now, you had a Chlorpactin treatment just last week. They usually take a while to work." Chlorpactin was a caustic chemical placed in the bladder to treat patients with interstitial cystitis. IC is a chronic painful bladder condition seen almost entirely in women. Chlorpactin required anesthesia during the installation because of intense pain. Julie suffered from this IC condition but enjoyed being treated this way.

"You have a tiny bug on your jacket!" Julie reached over and grasped something on Jackson's coat sleeve. She tossed that something onto the floor. "Dr. Cooper, please help. Can't a girl get attention here?"

•   •   •   •   •

The poster announced the annual Labor Day urology barbeque in September. The departmental event was at noon at the Kenneth George Bolton ranch in Portola Valley. Carl Washington was interested. The department only footnote did not dissuade him. Because of his status as a long-term patient, he felt that the department expected Carl's presence. The one problem with the poster was lacking a phone number or address. That was fine. He would inquire within.

Carl wheeled himself along the hallway. Since the urology clinic waiting room was not full, Carl wouldn't have a long wait. Soon, a nurse ushered him to an exam room for a brief wait.

"Mr. Washington, I am Dr. Cooper. How have you been?" Carl was a 53-year-old black male, T-7, thoracic level paraplegic. As with most spinal cord injury patients, he had a paralyzed bladder. He managed that by self-catheterizing four times daily.

"Dr. Cooper, so nice to meet you. I am doing well. I haven't had a bladder infection in years. I used to pass stones, but it's been a while. I am cathing regularly. I had an IVP last week. Is it all right?" Here, an x-ray of the kidneys with dye was obtained.

"I saw your IVP. It looks good. No stones, and the kidneys drain well. You had blood work last week. Your creatinine and blood count are fine." Serum creatinine is a measure of kidney function.

Jackson examined the patient and began wrapping up with him. "So, you are stable, and doing well, Mr. Washington. Let's plan on seeing you with x-rays and blood in six months."

"You should call me Carl." There was an uncomfortable pause. Out of respect, Jackson did not call patients by their first names. "How is your day, Dr. Cooper?" Carl, happy with his check-up, seemed to want more.

Jackson had already stood to leave. He smiled politely. "I am doing well. Busy as usual, but doing well. Thank you for asking, Mr. Washington."

"Do you have kids?"

Jackson glanced at the floor. "No. I am not married."

"Doesn't seem to matter to kids anymore. When injured in Vietnam, they told me I wouldn't have any kids. They were right. You know I have a new van. You can see it through that window." Carl pointed to the window. He turned his chair and moved to look out. Sitting in the distant parking lot was a new white Ford Transit.

"Nice, Mr. Washington." Jackson glanced at his wristwatch.

"Ya. It is roomy. I bunk in it, so it is nice. Say, that barbeque, where is the Kenneth George Bolton ranch? I know Portola Valley. Is it off Alhambra by the river?"

"I don't know. I haven't gone before. This is my first year. However, I believe it's only for staff. I am on call. Might not be there." Jackson sensed a loneliness in the man. He had no children, but did he have anyone? That comment: he bunks in there. Does Carl live in his van? Would he really come to the barbecue? The resident understood it as a departmental affair.

"Ya. Oh, that is too bad. What time on Saturday? Maybe you could give me the phone number? They did not list one or an address. Would the clinic receptionist know?"

"Sarah? Well, she might know." Jackson began to feel frantic. He looked at his watch again. His visit with Mr. Washington was going on for thirty minutes. He had so much to do.

"Dr. Cooper. Should I cath with a 14 French catheter still? I use the red rubber ones. Is that okay?"

"Yes. That will work. We will see you in six months." Jackson turned and left the room.

•   •   •   •   •

The Martin Luther King Jr. student pool was on the university campus, next to the Dwight D. Eisenhower Amphitheater. It was open to students, house staff, and other staff daily from noon to six p.m. The pool was an Olympic size of 50 meters and possessed one and three-meter diving boards.

Lee W. Hickok made use of the pool daily. Besides his vigorous lap swimming, springboard diving was his passion. He was an AAU medal diving champion from his days in Texas. Sweet Amber had not been on his menu yet.

It was a beautiful day as Lee W. finished his swim workout. Now he could concentrate on his favorite pastime. He began with several simple forward dives. Soon Lee W. completed a few backward and inward dives. He finished with a reverse, twisting, one-and-a-half rotation dive. When finished, there was quiet applause.

As he hurried to the locker room, one in the audience was particularly interesting to Lee W. She was lying on a lounge chair and gave an excellent, vigorous clap as he passed. Lee W. stopped and smiled. "Y'all are so nice." The man walked over to the girl. He pulled up a chair and sat. "I am Lee W. What's your name, honey?"

"Sadie. You're from the south, right Lee W.? I can tell by your accent. Where did you learn to dive so well?" Sadie was a woman of unusual beauty. She had thick blond hair tied in a medium-length ponytail that cascaded over her golden-tanned back. Her blue eyes sparkled, her complexion was like milk. The girl's smile was like an MTV model. Outfitted in a simple red two-piece bathing suit, she lay prone on her stomach on the lounge chair covered with a white and red towel.

"Texas, and yes, that is the south. Sadie."

CHAPTER 15

Labor Day broke beautifully, with a clean, warming sun and a delicate cloud cover. A gentle breeze wafted over the three-acre parcel of prime Portola Valley real estate. The so-called Kenneth George Bolton Ranch, owned and occupied by its namesake, spread out over rolling knolls and beautifully landscaped vales. Brick masonry paths and lovely finished patios circled the property in a meandering fashion.

The primary residence was a gray, angular, and modern-appearing barn with full-length picture windows looking out over the stylish property. A dark brick fireplace on the north wall spewed a peaceful, smokey discharge. A long circular brick driveway directed the guests to enter.

The site filled with interesting people: physicians, nurses, students, their spouses, and friends. The urology department and the entire medical center had a strong presence. People were meeting and mulling in groups spread over the entire property.

Kenneth George Bolton exited the Barn with an iced cup of C and a whim full of vigor. He stood looking over his palatial property. He wore a white tennis outfit with a knit polo shirt accented with narrow red and blue pinstripes. The shorts were surprisingly short, his round white varicose-laden legs exposed for the party to see. Kathryn exited the Barn and moved to his side. She, too, dressed in white tennis garb armed with a stylish patriotic colored skirt.

A high-pitched honk announced a Texas arrival. It was the first return day after the retrieval of Lee W. Hickok's ill-fated 240 Z's theft and stripping. After nearly two months in the body shop, the Z Car returned painted, straightened, restored, washed, waxed, and detailed.

Lee W. helped a pretty young companion from the passenger seat. She had a photogenic face framed by beautiful thick blond hair pulled back in a side-high ponytail, secured with a black and white polka-dotted scrunchy. Her shining blue eyes and white smile were memorable. Dressed in a sparkling silver low-cut blouse, white high-waisted pants, and red high-heeled pumps, the girl and her ample bosom were a sight to remember.

Lee W. turned and admired his Z Car as he walked toward the party. Dressed in a white T-shirt with the word TEXAS on the front, acid-washed jeans, and his signature red, white, and blue cowboy boots, the two looked like a Hollywood package.

Elmer James Crabb and Eleanor Jane Crabb arrived in a long black Mercedes limousine with fenders trimmed by small flying Old Glory. They exited the carriage with the doorman's help. She wore a pale blue floral wrap-around housedress and those common-sense lace-up Oxford shoes. Retrieving her black satchel from the car floor, she stumbled momentarily but quickly regained her footing. The professor emeritus was in a red, white, and blue sports coat, white slacks, and shiny polished brogues. A hand-tied red, white, and blue bowtie completed the picture.

Lee W. and his date made their way to the Barn. KGB and Kathryn were busy barking out instructions to the hired help. Soon they noticed the couple's presence and turned, shaking hands and exchanging names.

"Why, dear. It is so nice to have you here in Portola Valley. What is your name?"

"Sadie, Dr. Bolton. Sadie. Sadie Shinebright."

"You most certainly do, my dear." KGB then laughed loudly, punctuated with audible snorts. He glanced at her bosom, smiled, and then turned to his wife. "Sadie and Lee W., may I present my long-suffering wife, Kathryn?"

The four exchanged another round of polite handshakes and formal hugs. Sadie, carrying an Adidas water bottle, took a long drink. A man dressed in a white and black referee shirt, carrying a tray of shrimp HORS D'oeuvre, stopped and offered some to the group.

"I suggest you try these morsels. They are mighty fine." KGB grabbed a handful. The others used small plastic plates, dishing out the shrimp and eating politely.

"Are there any peanuts in the shrimp sauce?" Kathryn enquired nervously. She had a long history of violent peanut-related allergic reactions with anaphylaxis. Just last year, Patrice, at her favorite Chinese restaurant, had to resuscitate and intubate the woman. She was taking no chances. She politely declined the shrimp.

Patrice and Jackson ran a bit late as they journeyed from the hospital to Portola Valley in Patrice's Toyota. She turned onto Alhambra, by the river, and stopped at the light behind a new white Ford Transit van with disabled plates.

"I'll be damned! That is Carl Washington's van. I am certain. He's actually coming to the barbeque." Seeing him turn into the circular driveway at the Barn confirmed the suspicion.

Jackson and Patrice stood and waited for Carl Washington as he exited his van. He used a motorized ramp and quickly made his way over to the two. "Dr. Cooper, nice to see you again."

"Mr. Washington, meet Dr. Patrice Summers."

Carl shook her hand vigorously. "Call me Carl, Dr. Summers. Such a nice day, isn't it?"

Tara Patel was late as well. An early morning gunshot wound involving the kidney had occurred, and she was just leaving the hospital. She drove with the intern, Mike Nelson, in her old Honda Civic hatchback and made her way to Portola Valley. "Are you hungry, Mike? I am famished. Let's walk up there. Over there, by the smokey area. I think that is where they are cooking on the barbeque. Everyone is here. The place is getting busy."

Tara was right. Since noon, over one hundred UMC personnel had crowded onto KGB's property. The circular driveway was full of vehicles. People were milling around the ranch. There was talking and laughing.

A vast, smoking black barbeque stove stood in the middle of the property. Hired personnel were busy cooking hamburgers, dogs, and ribs. Tara arrived and looked hungrily on. Lee W. and Sadie surprised her from behind.

"Lee W., you scared me."

"Tara, this is Sadie. Sadie, this is Dr. Tara Patel, our esteemed chief resident. This here beach bum is Dr. Mike Nelson, the intern on her service." Lee W. jostled and rubbed Mike's straw-colored head of hair. He put out his arm and shook the intern's hand firmly. He then hugged Tara.

"Sadie, so nice to meet you. I like your scrunchy." Tara shook Sadie's hand. She brought her ever present water bottle to her lips and drank deeply.

"You're so cute, Dr. Patel. I mean, for a doctor, that is. I love your boots." The group looked at Tara's feet. She wore a pair of lace-up black Doc Martens.

"I got them from a stiff in the morgue." A hush came over the group. "I am just kidding."

Sadie laughed and laughed. She chortled impolitely and took another swig from her water bottle. "Wherever you got them, Tara, they sure are nice. What happened to my shoe?" The group looked down at Sadie. She stood on one red pump and one bare foot, her bright red toenails swinging in the breeze. The second shoe was nowhere to be seen. "Oh well, I have so many shoes."

A waitress swung by the Crabb's. EJC was engaged in a discussion with several medical students and house staff. "You are all a bunch of accommodated broods. Residents should live in the hospital. Indentured bonds are what we called it in my day."

"Would you care for an HORS d'oeuvre, Ma'am?"

Eleanor took a lump of meat wrapped in bacon. She put it in her mouth. She spat the HORS d'oeuvre into her hand and placed it back on the tray. As the waiter moved away, she swung her purse, hitting him on his rear. "Bring me a beer, monsignor."

"Y'all, dinner is served. If you progress to the firepit, these fine gentlemen will assist you presently. Have a nice chow." KGB set down the microphone. The chairman then walked to the barbeque and started a serving line. Scattered across the property were round, white plastic tables and chairs. With their food in hand, the guests began separating into groups.

KGB and Kathryn made their way to the head table, with plates capped with barbequed meats, salads, and dessert. Colleagues and staff soon sat at the table surrounding them. Carl Washington wheeled up, set down his plate, and ate. "Dr. Bolton, Carl Washington from Awalt U. Any chance of acquiring an extracorporeal shock wave lithotripter soon?" Carl was inquiring about a kidney stone shock wave system.

"The lithotripter is on its way as we speak. Who, by the way, are you, sir? Awalt U? Isn't that Awalt High School"

Carl continued feeding his face. He quickly changed the subject. "The ribs are delicious, group. Try the chicken, as well."

One guest took over the floor. "Dr. Bolton. Kathryn. Tell us about your beautiful home."

KGB began waxing about his favorite topic, the Kenneth George Bolton Ranch, as a light sprinkle began.

Lee W., Sadie, Tara, Jackson, Patrice, and Mike sat at the adjacent table. They all had full plates and were eating away. "Lee W., you use too much salt. Where is the pepper?" Sadie instructed the Texan on vital lessons of life. She took sip after sip on her water bottle and began gorging herself on the fine cuisine. "I have to have pepper, honey." She stood and collected a shaker from the adjacent table. When she returned, she misjudged the edge of her chair and sprawled on the ground. What she said was quite un-ladylike.

"Let me get you up, Sadie." Mike stood, pushing away his chair. He reached for the woman and pulled her upright.

"Whoops. Must have been the potato salad." She belched quietly behind her hand as she sat at the table with her pepper shaker.

A crack of thunder boomed overhead. Rain started pouring, and soon everyone got drenched, leaving their plates and seeking shelter under the trees and the two covered porches surrounding the Barn.

The rain did not bother EJC, for he was in full gear, leading a discussion at another table. While consuming his meal, the professor pontificated on his favorite subject for the group. It was, as always, the degradation of medical care by antibiotics. "When penicillin arrived in March 1945, it destroyed the future of medicine. No surgeon knows how to perform an adequate appendectomy anymore. The use of the surgical drain is a dying art, class."

"Bubba, where's that domestic when you need one? My ribs are cold."

"Not now, Bubbie. This is serious. This group is oblivious to the facts."

Eleanor began turning in her chair. She spied a server who made the mistake of coming to her aid.

"Can I help you, Madame?"

"Don't aggrandize me, Figaro. My ribs feel cold." She stood with difficulty and fell back, landing on her face in the muddy grass. She did not move, but began groaning in a high-pitched moan. "Oh, my leg. You loser! You moron! You pushed me."

•   •   •   •   •

Like many approaching their nineties, hip fractures are common. Osteoporosis with brittle bones is a fact of nature. The incidence in the ninth decade is high. The mortality for 90-year-old females is roughly 40%.

The party that day was over. Rain continued relentlessly for hours. The emergency medical technicians put a quell over the group. Many scattered back to their responsibilities in the hospital. Jackson was on call that night. Patrice was not and could go home for a few hours of much-needed sleep. Mike was due in the emergency room. UMC urology chief resident Tara Patel was on call, of course, a 24-7, seven-day-a-week responsibility.

On March 15, 1945, US pharmacies made penicillin available as an over-the-counter medication. The following year, Ernst Chain and Howard Florey won the Nobel Prize for their work on the drug. Experts seldom question that the ensuing antibiotic era was responsible for significant advances in modern medicine.

CHAPTER 16

Jackson recognized the surgery preop number from his pager. "This is Dr. Cooper. I was paged." It was early Monday morning, a full day of surgeries ahead for the resident. He was in the cafeteria, trying for a coffee and a muffin.

"Julie Mc Sweeney is in preop, doctor."

Julie Mc Sweeney? The name instilled fear in his thoughts. Jackson pulled his OR list from his scrub pocket, scanning for her name. The first case was a cystoscopy with Chlorpactin installation for interstitial cystitis, or IC, on a patient named Julie Mc Sweeney. Seeing her name, he remembered more than he wanted about the patient.

"You wanted to see her before surgery."

The nurse on the phone was nice, but probably inexperienced. He didn't require a pre-surgery patient examination. He would do the case and see the family in the waiting room. She was staying overnight. He would see the patient on the ward during afternoon rounds. "What do you mean? What's your name?"

"Cindy. Doctor. Julie says you wanted to talk to her before she went to the OR. She is very nice. But I don't know. Did you tell her that?"

"Of course not. Well, Mc Sweeney is, well, let's just say, odd, Cindy."

"Tell me about it." The nurse seemed to want to unload her Mc Sweeney experiences at Jackson. "Ms. Mc Sweeney has a big purse stuffed with supplies. I think she stole them. I swear she took my penlight."

Jackson laughed to himself. Would the patient have the last laugh? He wondered. He recalled the patient's large stuffed purse in the clinic. Jackson felt an odd, suspicious feeling about Ms. Mc Sweeney. Despite his reservations, he instructed the nurse to inform her he would see her in the operating room before she falls asleep.

Jackson walked into OR room two. Unlike room six, they designated this room for minor cases. In room six, the chief resident and urology attendings performed major cases, often cancer-related. Room two belonged to the junior resident. Here he would spend the day doing his cases.

"Hi, Dr. Cooper. I am so glad you are here." Julie was lying on the operating table under a warm blanket, smiling and waving at Jackson. Her stretchy surgical hat and lack of makeup made her look like a ripe tomato with a slightly odd face.

Jackson apprehensively walked up to the table. The girl grabbed his hand seductively, holding on firmly. He freed his arm and gently pulled his hand away. "Ms. Mc Sweeney, you're okay. You should go to sleep now." The girl stared at Jackson with trembling blue eyes. Within seconds, they closed, and the patient was asleep.

Jackson and Chris, the new intern, walked down the W3B hallway to Mr. Simpson's room. He wanted to instruct Chris on securing a catheter with tape. Mr. Simpson was a post-op Camay procedure. In that procedure, the surgeon removed the bladder and prostate for cancer, and constructed an artificial bladder. They left a catheter in the penis. Dislodging it would precipitate a surgical emergency. The tube needed to be secured daily with fresh tape.

"Doctor Cooper." Mabel was an older, very experienced nurse who rushed to see Jackson. She seemed frustrated with something of note to report. "Julie Mc Sweeney says you wanted to see her ASAP. I don't know. Dr. Cooper, could you see her for just a second? She is very persistent. Actually, sort of weird. She sure sucks up the morphine. A lot of pain, I imagine."

"How much morphine, Mabel?"

"Let's see. I gave Mc Sweeney six mg IM when she arrived about two hours ago. Then she got two doses of two mg IV. She still wants more."

"Don't give her anymore, Mabel. Chris, could you see her after Mr. Simpson? I will see her on afternoon rounds. I wish we could discharge her. Tara says Chlorpactin's stay overnight, though." One advantage of being the resident is that he could delegate. Chris, the intern, was in for an uncomfortable experience.

Julie Mc Sweeney was in the hospital for four whole days. The doctors instituted a rule-out myocardial infarction or heart attack workup because of Julie McSweeney's complaints of chest pain. Because of shortness of breath, the medical staff enforced a rule-out pulmonary embolus, or blood clot in the lung, protocol. The complaints of right-sided paralysis required a workup for cerebral vascular accident or stroke. The medical staff evaluated all these symptoms with multiple tests, examinations, and physician consults.

The patient continued with her demanding, manipulative behavior. Her overlying personality was needy. Multiple medical evaluations revealed no significant abnormalities.

•   •   •   •   •

Jerome "Buzzy" Whitmore continued in critical condition in the surgical ICU. Fever started on day one after surgery. It concerned Patrice, for the surgery was dirty and contaminated. Colonic contents splashed all over the abdomen because of the gunshot wound. It was Patrice's first big case as a junior resident, and she took pride in the outcome. The doctor did not appreciate the looming sepsis with a fever.

The attempt on Buzzy's life precipitated significant changes to security. A police officer, complete with a firearm, sat at the door. The staff welcomed their presence. Security patrolled the ward and the nursing station.

Buzzy possessed a large circle of family and acquaintances who requested access. Most were acceptable, some very shady. The staff encouraged a select group. It was the 1980s when seeing family members were thought to help a patient's recovery. One person at a time could see Buzzy during visiting hours.

"Mr. Buzzy, I am going to do your dressing change." Patrice took down the abdominal dressing after morphine pre-med. She inspected his open mid-line abdominal wound, satisfied with its progress. Patrice then cleansed the wound and applied Betadine wet to dry dressings. Here, she packed the wound with gauze soaked in iodine soap. The purpose was to cleanse and debride the wound by removing adherent gauze with each dressing change.

"I know it is painful, Mr. Buzzy. I need to do this q 6." Patrice would return every six hours for this procedure.

As she left the room, she noticed the absence of the police officer. Where was the man? She wondered. On a hunch, she checked the staff lounge. There he was, smoking a cigarette and drinking a cup of coffee. "Officer Quick. I am a little worried. The room. It is open, and Buzzy is by himself." The officer nodded, quenched his cigarette, and returned to the room.

The ICU waiting room was alive with activity. Buzzy's extended family was moving in. Many characters sat in chairs. Blankets were strewn around, and several visitors lay on the floor. There was social chatter, with laughing and often loud arguments. A wall-mounted television blared, The Gong Show spewing insanity.

Hector was the man in charge. The gangster sat brooding in a corner chair, licking his gold tooth. He smoked cigarette after cigarette, his ashtray heaped over with buds falling to the floor. Again, he dressed brightly. Today in a yellow and black Adidas tracksuit and matching sneakers, with a bright yellow skull cap. "Tyesha, get me a brew."

Tyesha responded quickly. She fetched a cold Budweiser from the cooler on the floor for him. "All the dudes seen Buzz 'cept me."

While the guilty individual that shot Buzzy in the abdomen two days ago was in custody, intrigue was still afoot. An attempt on Buzzy's life in the ICU occurred yesterday. They held Tooty responsible. "Y'all gots to tell 'em, hoe. You'se need to see the Buzz." Hector popped open the beer. With a disgusted expression, he scanned the room. "What you care, Bitch."

Tyesha behaved as community property. Relationships were a natural part of her character. By right, she was Hector's possession. Hector doubted her loyalty.

Nurse Brittany returned to the ICU waiting room. She looked about the room. Tyesha jumped up and spoke to the nurse. "I needs to see Buzz next."

"You are next. Here, put on this coverup." Brittany handed the scantily clad Tyesha a yellow open gown and led the girl down the hall to Buzzy's room.

"Here, sign here." The police officer stood with a clipboard and a pen. He indicated all visitors need to sign in.

Tyesha scribbled just a large X. Then someone led her to the bedside. Loud crying and tears began as soon as the girl saw Buzzy. It was like a waterwork flow, with moaning and the production of tears that covered her face, smeared her makeup, and even flowed over her snake tattooed neck. Guilt was apparent amid romantic feelings for the unconscious man.

When she returned to the waiting room, Tyesha was still crying. She wiped her face and entered the room. She then quickly moved to sit alone in the corner.

"Who wishes to see the patient next?" Brittany explained it was nearly the end of visiting hours. One more person, and the room closes for the night.

Hector got up. He extinguished the cigarette and finished the Bud can. Brittany directed him through the hallway. The police officer was curiously absent from the room's entry. Brittany tried unsuccessfully to get Hector to sign on the clipboard. He refused and walked to the bedside.

Buzzy was still ventilator bound. There was a tube in his throat, a nasogastric tube in his nostril, and his hands secured to the bedside. His belly-bound colostomy bag lay empty.

"Where is Officer Quick?" Brittany put down an IV bag, turned, and walked to the door. She searched the lounge for him.

Hector moved to the bedside. He stared at the empty colostomy bag and began chuckling. "A shit bag! Got your shit bag. You got your dues, dude." He pulled a large, dark, liquid-containing syringe from his jacket. He uncapped the needle and slowly injected the substance through Buzzy's IV.

In a flash, Officer Quick seized the man. He grabbed the rest of the syringe and forced it away. Seizing Hector's jacket, he swiftly brought him down, landing on top.

Amidst their struggle, Brittany took the syringe from the officer's hand. She activated the room's alarm, and soon personnel surrounded them.

Patrice was in the nursing station, readying herself for another round of wound changes. When the alarm went off, she ran to the room. The officer was pulling Hector to his feet. He forced his hands behind him, placing him in cuffs. The crowded room, filled with personnel, moved to the bedside and questioned Hector's actions.

Patrice took the syringe. She squeezed out a drop of the brown liquid onto a gloved fingertip. One smell told her all she needed to know. "Stool!"

Patrice put a page in for her chief resident in the nurse's lounge. James Tyrone soon called back. "I am sure it is a 60-cc syringe full of liquified stool, James."

"How much did he infuse?"

"Around 50 cc remains, perhaps 10."

"Culture the stool. What antibiotic is he on?"

"Ampicillin, Flagyl, and gentamycin."

"That should cover it, Patrice. Watch Buzzy closely for signs of sepsis."

James then hung up the phone. Another attempt on the patient's life occurred. This time, it was ingenious. If Hector had infused an entire syringe of liquefied stool, the incredible bacterial contamination would have likely induced a high fever, septic shock, and death. The ingenious part was that the source of his sepsis would have been unknown. Hector could have disappeared into the hospital, while his nemesis would die from sepsis of unknown origin.

CHAPTER 17

Eleanor Crabb was as dreadful a terror on the ward as she was everywhere else. Orthopedics treated her femoral neck fracture the night of the departmental barbeque with surgical exploration and hip replacement. Following ICU, she moved to W3B under the care of an unsuspecting orthopedist. She did well clinically, but intimidated anyone and everyone who was involved in her care.

Eleanor yelled into the television remote. "Will one of you creatures bother enough to bring the bedpan? I have to pee. Now! I'm going to gush like a firehose. Hello! Any of you peons home?" As she yelled, she spit, her dentures residing on the nightstand. The belligerent woman's bladder was draining fine, catheterized, her urinary output flowing freely into the bag.

Nurse Sally's unfortunate assignment tonight was attending to Mrs. Crabb's hospital care. The nurse knocked quietly and timidly opened the room door. "Mrs. Crabb. Are you all right?" She asked fearfully. "Are you trying to call us? No, that is the TV control. Let's give you the call button." She removed the remote and placed the call button in Eleanor's wrinkled hand. "Just talk clearly. The speaker will pick up your voice, Mrs. Crabb." Sally reached down and emptied the Foley bag. "You are peeing great."

"And that is where you are wrong, cookie. I'm going to piddle like a water fountain. Get out of my way." Eleanor sat up and kicked the nurse in the belly.

Sally stumbled back, startled. Eleanor struggled to rise from bed. "The catheter. You don't need to pee. Let it out, Mrs. Crabb."

There was a knock on the door. Eleanor yelled out. "Enter my domicile, Renfield."

Elmer Crabb shuffled into the room. "Bubbie, what is the help doing to you?"

With the name Bubbie, a total change came over Eleanor. She smiled and sat up. She moistened a finger and traced her lips as if applying makeup. The woman pulled her free leg onto the bed and freshened the bed sheet. "Bubba, this lowly domestic assaulted me. But never you mind." She said, turning to Sally. "Okay, Crumpet. Bring us our cups. It is teatime."

•   •   •   •   •

When Jackson saw her name, he felt sick. Here she was, Julie Mc Sweeney, in the clinic for a post-op visit. The woman was bizarre. Was she a borderline personality? Was she a Munchhausen? These diagnoses were for the psych department, not urology. His interest in these conditions was nonexistent. However, Mc Sweeney was Jackson Cooper's problem again.

She sat on the floor, dressed in bright pink pajamas and furry cat slippers. A red Minnie Mouse beanie was on her head. She had applied her thick makeup once again. To Jackson, she looked like a red cream éclair.

"Dr. Cooper, I am in horrible pain. The Vicodin is not helping. My bladder feels simply nuclear. Did you rupture me? It is going to fall out. That happened to my friend, Gloria. What did you do in there? Did you leave an atomic fireball inside my bladder?"

"A Chloropactin installation, Ms. Mc Sweeney. You know about this. You've had maybe ten before."

"Never like this. I'm not sure you even did my operation. I need a morphine shot. Why did you send me home from the hospital like that?"

•   •   •   •   •

A note from Membership Services was in his message box at lunchtime. *Please call about Julie Mc Sweeney.*

On rounds that afternoon, Tara Patel confronted Jackson. "Jackson, you got to move on when you are in the clinic. Julie Mc Sweeney is a manipulative, needy IC whacko. I sent her home with some Percocet after you left her in clinic." Tara was sort of mad at Jackson. She felt he had fallen prey to a pathologic woman. She felt that her admission with all the consultations was very naïve of him. "Handle these patients quickly, Jackson."

•   •   •   •   •

"This is Dr. Cooper. I was paged."

"Hi, Dr. Cooper. This is Carol Barkley. I am on the oncology service. We have a patient named Clay Michaels who's getting Cis-Platinum for testis cancer. He has retroperitoneal fibrosis (RPF) from radiotherapy. Your department put stents in him a while back. He urinates often, day and night in fact. Is there something you could do for the poor guy?"

Jackson was familiar with the patient. He saw him in the GU-Oncology clinic several weeks ago. During the late 1970s, he received treatment for testicular cancer through surgery and radiation. He was receiving Cis-Platinum chemotherapy for a recurrence of cancer in his lungs. In addition, he had RPF, scar tissue in the abdomen, and obstruction of both ureters because of previous radiation therapy. Stents are small plastic tubes that hold the ureters open. The patient had one in each of his ureters. They irritate the bladder, giving urinary frequency.

"You got him on Ditropan?" The drug is a bladder relaxant that helps reduce bladder frequency.

"Yes, but he has severe dry mouth from it. It didn't help, anyway."

"Carol, nothing else will help." Jackson hung up before the girl could speak. He was tired as usual, but in a distressed condition. His Tic Tacs were not the answer anymore.

A message on his answering machine from his sister had just said she wanted to talk to him about Thomas.

Thomas Fetterling was his good friend from medical school. He was an orthopedic resident at Brown University. He was not doing well. When Jackson recently spoke to him, he was distraught, tired, and defeated. The topic of suicide came up. Jackson talked to him. He tried to boost the man's spirits, but Jackson felt similarly. A similar phone call last year was about Adam DeWalt, a cardio-thoracic resident at Tufts. His sister informed him that Adam hung himself in the surgery call room on Christmas day. Jackson could not handle this.

Patrice was off call when he called her. He hoped she was in her apartment. "Leave a message, and I will get back to you." Her absence was unfortunate.

Lee W. was in his office. He paged Jackson and asked him to come to see him. "Jackson, what is the matter, big buddy?"

"I don't know Lee W. I am just worn. What's up?"

"I hate to get into this, y'all. Do you know Dr. Carol Barkley? She's one of the oncology attendings. Real nice, but sort of stickler. Did she consult you about Clay Michaels?"

Jackson's heart began to race. He knew what Lee W. was getting at. Was that Carol an attending? Mistakenly, he believed she was a medical student. He should have given her more assistance. He shouldn't have been so curt with her. He should have seen the patient. Perhaps one of his stents had migrated. Replacement could have cured his bladder irritation and resulting frequency. "Yes. What about him?"

"Well, she called me this afternoon. She was very upset. She says you wouldn't talk to her. I went up to the ward. Jackson, the guy's stent, has migrated. It was hanging out of his penis. The diagnosis was easily made. I removed it. Let's replace it in the morning."

Jackson sat down, his head in his hands. Despite his efforts, he was close to tears. "Lee W., I am sorry. I was a butt. I never realized she was an attending." As he said that, he recalled being a medical student. Student or not, he should have seen the patient. "I'll schedule him for tomorrow."

"Not enough, Jackson. She wants an apology. Could you call her right away?"

•   •   •   •   •

Jackson Cooper could not sleep again. He looked at his alarm clock with sadness. The night would soon be over. Patrice was asleep next to him. He turned and fondly looked at her. She seemed so peaceful, something that always eluded him. Their time together tonight, as always, was beautiful, but too short. Soon, they will be back at the demanding hospital grind, toiling from dusk till dawn. He desired to heal others, yet could never heal himself.

Their meal tonight included a delicious New York strip steak grilled on the little Hibachi on his front porch. Patrice cooked wild rice and tossed a Caesar salad. A bottle of Cabernet Sauvignon finished it perfectly.

Jackson rose quietly. He exited the bedroom, shut the door, and settled on the sofa. He was so tired but couldn't sleep. Jackson was unwilling to call his sister back today. Thomas Fetterling's fate would have to wait. He couldn't handle another tragedy.

Jackson felt that slight sense of nausea in the pit of his stomach. It reminded him of his narcotic addiction and the withdrawals that consumed him last year. He longed for a fix. He knew by experience the effect. It would temporarily resolve his melancholy and give him some of the strength that he needed to continue.

Jackson stood and moved to the hallway closet. Hidden on the shelf was his secret desire. His nemesis and close friend lay again in the old white sock, overpowering his will. Only one drop in the syringe. However, it was Fentanyl, the most potent narcotic in the world. He was no longer tolerant to the drug like last year. A drop would send him away on the journey.

Jackson moved to the couch. He exposed his left forearm, wrapping the tourniquet around his arm. The opening of the door stopped him. He quickly removed the tight rubber band and stuffed all the paraphernalia behind a pillow.

"Jackson, come back to bed." Patrice stood looking at him with concern. She wore his white T-shirt, the one from Lee W. with Texas scrolled across the front. It was a gift from one addict to another to celebrate their one year of sobriety.

"I couldn't sleep, Patrice. It's okay. I love you."

Patrice sat on the couch. She wrapped a comforter around her shoulders and kissed him on the cheek. "Do you have any left, Jackson?"

It didn't surprise Jackson. He knew she would know. He also wanted to be rid of it. Jackson cried. He stopped himself and wiped his eyes.

Jackson pulled the paraphernalia out and handed it to Patrice. "There is just a drop left. I was thinking of using. Take this away, Patrice."

"I will, Jackson. But you need to take away its attraction. There is always another dose. Why do you always want it?"

That was the question. For so long, Jackson's solution to stress was chemical escape. He lost the ability to escape on his own when he took that first Percocet tablet. It made him feel whole, but never satisfied. "What can I do?" Jackson knew the correct answer.

"I would pray, Jackson. Remember, in Philippians. I think it is 4:13. I can do all things through Christ who strengthens me."

The prayer that night was simple. Jackson asked Christ to renew his strength against the temptation of pharmakeia, or chemical sorcery. He had prayed for that before. It would not be the last time.

CHAPTER 18

Wei Huan could see the finish line. He felt he was close, hopefully going home this week. Surgery removed the staghorn stone, with Renacidin irrigation used to dissolve any residue stones. Now, the task was to prove the kidney's cleanliness and absence of fragments. Today he would have nephrotomograms of his left kidney, x-rays that focused on the inside of the organ, looking for stones.

Wei was scooting on his board in the hallway when he crossed paths with the rounding urologists. "Mr. Huan, how are you this morning?" Tara Patel, Jackson, and the rest of the team stopped and circled the patient. His nephrostomy tube was draining clear volumes of urine. A small heparin lock IV in his hand replaced the prior neck IV.

"I am doing very well. Thank you, Dr. Patel. What is the plan for today? When can I be discharged?"

"Another set of nephrotomograms today. If they are free of fragments, we clamp your tube. If you tolerate that for 24 hours, you're home!" Tara turned to the new intern. "Chris, make sure you cover the procedure."

"Chris scribbled down a note on his clipboard." A dose of intravenous antibiotics would treat any infection on the nephrostomy tube, termed covering with antibiotics. An order in the chart to the nurses was required.

Jackson Cooper was in radiology observing Wei's nephrotomograms. The x-rays showed no residual stone fragments. Jackson felt a modicum of pride. The case was the most significant of his career. With excitement, he visualized presenting the nephrotomograms in the departmental meeting tomorrow. If EJC was present, even the gruff old fart might be happy.

Jackson put on a small clamp occluding the nephrostomy tube. With that clamped, it forced all urine to drain down the ureter into his stoma bag ileal conduit. If successful, they could remove the tube the next day.

• • • • •

"This is Dr. Cooper. I was paged?"

"Jackson, this is Chris. Mr. Latinsky's CD4 count is down again. It was 75 last week, but now it is 58." The CD4 count measured the number of T-cells in Mr. Latinsky's blood. T-cells are helper lymphocytes necessary in the immune system. The normal value is above 200 per cubic millimeter of blood.

"I didn't see him on morning rounds."

"He was in x-ray getting a chest x-ray."

"Let's swing by radiology and check it out."

"Joanne, do you have Maurice Latinsky's morning chest film?"

Joanne Miller was a radiologist. She was scanning x-rays on her large rotating view box. "What's his medical record number?"

Chris read off the eight-digit number.

"Okay, here is his film from one week ago." Joanne continued using her pocket pointer. "Well, he has an old Ghon complex. See the calcified hilar granuloma?" A Ghon complex is a chest x-ray finding in tuberculosis patients.

Chris told about the patient's history. "He has renal TB, so those are old chest x-ray findings."

Joanne continued. "Well, his old film is otherwise clear. Now, this morning's film shows significant changes. See the bilateral, diffuse, granular infiltrates. Does this patient have AIDS?" Maurice's chest x-ray from the past was stable. Today he had severe congestion in both lungs.

"Yes, Joanne. Mr. Latinsky is an AIDS patient."

"Well, the infiltrates are not from TB. This chest x-ray is consistent with pneumocystis pneumonia until proven different." Pneumocystis pneumonia is a lung infection from a fungus/protozoa seen primarily in AIDS patients. Joanne put down her pointer and sipped her cup of coffee. "I am sorry. He has progressed rapidly."

●   ●   ●   ●   ●

"The Krauts have got me! Let me go. You can't do that." Maurice Latinsky wrestled for his life in bed. With his feet, he kicked away the covers and struggled to stand.

Freddie spent the night sleeping in the bedside reclining chair. He sat up, startled, and tossed his comforter to the ground. "Maury, it is all right."

Maurice stared at the man with his wild wide heterochromatic eyes. He started coughing violently. What began last week as an occasional dry hack was now florid. Perspiration from his fever soaked his pajamas.

"Your cough, dear. It is getting so much worse. And you're soaked in sweat again." Freddie reached for the call button. When the ward clerk responded, he began crying. "My Maury, he's very sick."

Jackson came down from the call room. He entered the dark room with the night nurse. Maurice looked so ill on afternoon rounds; he looked even worse tonight. His cough was fierce. It was productive of blood-tinged sputum. Fever returned and he lost three more pounds. Today's chest x-ray was concerning.

The treatment of pneumocystis pneumonia involves an antibiotic called Septra, also known as Bactrim. Jackson intended to begin the patient on that, but it had to be postponed until the pulmonary service could perform a bronchoscopy and lung biopsy tomorrow morning.

"Maurice, you alright?" Jackson listened to his lungs, which were congested and junky. The nurse took his temperature. It was 101 degrees.

In the waiting room, Jackson sat down with Freddie. "He is not doing well, Mr. Bishop. His immune system is deteriorating. We know that from his CD4 count. It should be above 200. His was 58 this morning."

"He is coughing again, like before. Has his TB come back, doctor?"

"His TB seems okay, Freddie. We took that out with the surgeries. No, he looks to have pneumocystis pneumonia. It is an infection of the lungs. We see it almost always in patients with AIDS."

"Why don't you give him antibiotics?"

"We are going to. Be prepared, however. Septra, that's the antibiotic, is only partially effective in these settings. It doesn't work really well, unfortunately. But we can't start that until he has the bronchoscopy and lung biopsy tomorrow morning. The antibiotic would mask the results."

"What is? Did you say bronchoscopy?"

"Yes. A pulmonary doctor puts a telescope into the lungs for a piece of tissue and culture. They will sedate him. After that, we will give him Septra through his IV."

"Thank you, doctor."

"Freddie, he needs an isolation room. He will not like that."

Maurice tried desperately not to cough. Freddie was asleep in the chair. He didn't want to wake him. The man stood slowly at the bedside. He was lightheaded and dizzy, but it soon passed. From under the bed, Maurice pulled his helmet and cardigan. He looked once at his urinal and decided against it.

He slipped into slippers and padded his way down the dark hallway. He encountered a few people but received little attention.

The ducks were asleep, the fountains still launching their cool water into the air. A gentle breeze wafted over the pond. Maurice sat on the bench and thought. He knew he was going to die; it was just a matter of time. The past few months took a heavy toll on him. He did not think through that rushing car ride to the hospital. If Maurice had known, he would have declined. Everyone was wonderful at UMC, but the hospital itself was stifling. It was repressive. It was nothing more than a prison.

The scooter board echoed in the night. Maurice's note slipped under Wei's door was successful. His buddy arrived, determined to support his only friend.

"Hi, Maurice. Where are the ducks?"

"Sleeping. Ducks are so lucky. They can do whatever they want."

Wei took a deep breath of the clean air. "You're right, Maurice. It is nice down here. What are you going to do?"

Maurice began coughing. He covered his mouth with his sleeve. He took his helmet off when the spell resolved and handed it to his friend. "I want you to have this, Wei. It's all I have, not much. I am dying. It won't be long, my friend."

Wei looked Maurice over. The man was not really shocked. He knew of Maurice's diagnosis. He looked with sympathy at the wasted shell of his friend. Maurice was coughing and sputtering. He was short of breath and wheezing. His brow was wet with sweat. A newly raised purplish lesion was present on his nose. It looked like a raspberry but ominous and sad. You want to go back in, right? They have tests for you. Don't give up, Maurice. God doesn't want you to stop."

"Is there a God, Wei?"

Wei paused for a long time. "I believe so, Maury. Look at me. They say I get a new body in Heaven. I am counting on that."

There was a crowd in the nursing station when Wei brought Maurice back. Jackson was down from the call room. Tara swung by after a midnight surgical case. Chris, the intern, had just arrived. Nurses and staff stood and looked at the duo. The nurse led Maurice to the isolation room, closing the door slowly.

CHAPTER 19

The split-thickness skin graft (STSG) is an essential tool in the plastic surgeon's arsenal, designed to cover large areas of damaged tissue. Cam Thompson possessed extensive areas of damaged tissue. His face looked like shredded beef after his attempt on his life with a 12-gauge shotgun. It was time to cover that tissue to prevent infection and losing blood and vital bodily fluids.

Cam was on Patrice's General Surgery A service. She was in the plastic surgery program, now a junior resident on that service. She asked her chief resident for permission to perform an STSG on the patient. Dr. Tyrone felt her prior experiences were adequate and allowed her the opportunity.

An STSG transplants a large area of skin from a donor location, in this case Cam's thigh, onto distant areas.

"Marking pen." Patrice took a purple felt pen and traced out the intended donor site. "Dermatome." She then took the air-powered reciprocating knife and sliced off the graft. She then transferred harvested grafts onto the absent jaw, face, and right eye socket.

At the OR nursing station, a yellow sticky note with the name Dr. Summers waited for her. The nurse caught Patrice on the way to the post-anesthesia recovery room, handing her the message. "What's this, Kelley?"

"Dr. Winters called just after you started in room eight. He mentioned waiting until you finished in the OR."

Patrice read the brief note. *Buzzy is septic.*

Billie Winters was the Surgery A intern. When Patrice entered the ICU, he was busy placing a Swan-Ganz (SG) catheter into Buzzy's neck. Buzzy was the abdominal gunshot wound victim. The catheter, used to monitor heart pressures, was especially useful in cases of septic shock.

"Advance it a little more. I like to flick it like a dart, Billie." Billie was advancing the SG through the right ventricle into the pulmonary artery. To do so, Patrice suggested flicking the catheter, like throwing a dart. "There. That's it. It's wedged." The catheter was now in the correct position.

Buzzy developed a fever after Patrice's surgery. She believed the infection originated in the abdomen. It was a significantly contaminated, or dirty, surgical case. In addition to the damaged spleen, the left colon was blown apart. Stool was everywhere inside of the abdomen. A colostomy repaired the damage. Patrice profusely irrigated the belly with liters of sterile water. Despite this, the risk of abscess development was high. In addition, Hector had infused at least 10 cc of stool into his IV. All of this pointed to the development of sepsis.

Buzzy's blood pressure was low and unstable. His pulse was rapid, and ventilator values were abnormal. Very little urine was in his catheter. All of these factors pointed to sepsis caused by bacteria in the blood.

"He needs more fluids, Billie. His wedge pressure is low. What is his crit?"

"His hematocrit was 26 this morning."

"Give him two units of blood. Bolus him with normal saline as well. Begin dopamine at three mics." Dopamine was a drug used to raise blood pressure.

The two physicians were busy treating Buzzy's septic shock. Nurses were carrying out orders. Blood arrived from the Blood Bank. They established a drip of dopamine.

"Patrice, do you think some whacko injected stool into his IV again?" Billie asked what everyone was thinking.

Patrice sighed deeply. That question bothered her since Hector tried to inject a syringe of stool several days ago. He intended to bolus Buzzy with a large volume of significantly contaminated material. The result would be sepsis, shock, and, if enough succus, death. She couldn't grasp the psycho-dynamic in the waiting room.

The guard at the door was reading a newspaper. "Officer, has anyone come to see Buzzy?" Since the incident strict visitor restrictions were in place. Only hospital staff could see the patient. Patrice thought that Hector and Tooty were in custody. However, she had no opportunity to check.

The guard put down his paper. "Not that I am aware of, Dr. Summers. I just got here, though. Gonzales was on overnight." He picked up and started reading.

Buzzy was in Trendelenburg position, with his legs in the air. Despite wide open fluid infusion and rapid infusion of dopamine, his blood pressure was dangerously low. Buzzy started having an irregular heart tracing on the EKG. Soon, runs of worrisome arrhythmias began.

"Better give a dose of Amiodarone, Billie. Get 300 milligrams stat." The drug treated these arrhythmias. "V-Fib, call a code."

Buzzy was in cardiac arrest before the code team arrived. Billie jumped on his chest and began CPR.

"Stop CPR." Patrice was running the code. She had chest percussions stop to watch the cardiac tracing. "Flatline. Shock him. Clear."

There was a buzz hive, so to speak, in the room. In these situations, a near hysteria overcomes all involved. CPR involving chest percussions, manual ventilation through his breathing tube, intravenous drugs, and electro-cardioversion continued. Despite all these measures, Buzzy continued in cardiac arrest.

Patrice poured iodine soap over the chest. "Stop CPR." The cardiac arrest continued.

Cardiac surgery arrived. The female surgeon placed a surgical tray on the foot of the bed. She nodded to Patrice. The two then made an incision over the heart. Patrice massaged the heart for several minutes with a gloved hand on the ventricle. There was no pulse.

Patrice stepped away from the table. She felt defeated, with no options remaining. Buzzy's soul was catapulted into eternity as the team watched. "Stop CPR." Patrice looked sadly at her wristwatch. "Time of death, 2:40 AM."

The room cleared of personnel slowly. Patrice and Billie stood at the bedside, drained and sad. Nurses began cutting Buzzy free from IVs and tubes. They attempted to clean the patient, preparing for the removal of the body.

Patrice excused the officer and, with the chart, sat in his chair by the door. She carefully wrote a death note describing all the resuscitative measures. "Billie. You can take off. I just heard you paged overhead."

Patrice sighed as she watched the staff cleaning Buzzy and the room. She was exhausted and more so emotionally drained. Could she continue to practice medicine at this pace? Buzzy was the first of her own surgery cases to die. She saw many patients die, but never one she personally operated on. It was brutal and devastating to her. She stood, gazing directly at the patient. She felt suddenly ashamed. Patrice had never looked at him in the face directly.

Patrice wondered about the family. When she ran by the ICU several hours before, the waiting room was empty. Before leaving, now, she needed to verify.

He was sitting in the empty waiting room, staring at Patrice as she stood in the doorway. A sick smile came over his face, his gold-toothed mouth sucking on what appeared to be a joint. He gestured to the doctor with a Budweiser-containing hand. "How's Buzzy, Doc?"

"Dead, you vulture."

"Why so serious?"

"He didn't deserve to die like that, Hector."

"You didn't know the dude, Doc."

CHAPTER 20

Anthony Lorenzo Giordano was a high-powered San Francisco attorney. He became Kenneth George Bolton's urologic patient after his second sexually transmitted disease (STD) in the 1960s. The effective Penicillin treatment enamored the man to the chairman indefinitely. It was years since the last outbreak, coincidentally years since his divorce, that seemed to rid himself of the vexing urethral problem. However, he continued to see the chairman regularly, concerned with recurrence.

Because of Giordano's fame, he was strictly a private patient. When in KGB's clinic, signs of sequestration would appear. Residents were not allowed.

"Antony, how are you?"

"It is Anthony, Dr. Bolton, Anthony. Not Antony, I am fine. My pecker is fine. Between you and me, it came from my first wife. What a bitch. Glad she's gone."

KGB then evaluated the man. He performed a physical exam and microscopically examined his urine for infection. Then came the rectal exam. The chairman entertained the possibility of prostate cancer when he noted a prostate nodule.

"My postate, there is a lump in it?"

"You gotts a little tiny lump on the outside of your prostate. Y'all. It is probably nothing. I can biopsy you right now."

"Time is a wasting, Ken-boy."

•   •   •   •   •

With the biopsy positive for cancer, Anthony demanded the organ's removal. KGB was more than happy to arrange surgery, a radical prostatectomy.

When the day of Mr. Giordano's surgery arrived, residents were out of bounds. They discouraged traffic in the operating theatre. Paper covered the OR door windows. Signs indicated that this was a private affair.

KGB would be the primary surgeon but chose no resident as his assistant. The chairman selected Lee W. Hickok to assist. Only the chairman of the anesthesiology department, Ken Forling, held the anesthesia position. KGB handpicked three nurses to help during the case.

The surgery progressed acceptably. After removing the prostate, the team planned the anastomosis. Here, they sewed the stump of the urethra to the bladder. This is perhaps the most critical step. The urethral stump routinely retracted down into the pelvis. Putting sutures into this structure is difficult. KGB, via Lee W., had a trick to accomplish this.

"We are now going to perform a Hickok maneuver, Lee. W. Please, do so at your leisure."

"Ken, it is not a Hickok maneuver. I just came up with it. It sometimes helps, y'all."

The phone on the wall behind the anesthesiologist rang. Dr. Forling picked up the phone. "Hello. Who is this? Louise? Okay. He is right here. Ken, your ex-wife, Louise, is on the phone. She says it is very important."

KGB turned away from the operative field and stared at Dr. Forling. His beet-red face showed apparent anger. His glasses fogged as he spoke into the speakerphone: "Louise. What are you calling me here for? You know better."

"I am going to put you on speakerphone, Mrs. Bolton. Or I mean Louise."

"Kenny, you must take Gwendolen to the big island next month."

KGB was boiling. Holding a surgical clamp, he dropped it on the back table. "Louise, I am in the middle of a radical prostate. I am operating on a very important patient named Antony Giordano. Now what in the name of mercy causes y'all to call me here?"

"Gwendolen is distraught with you, in particular. You never talk to her. You never even call. You need to be with the girl. You know her menstrual periods are flowing like the Amazon because of that. She goes through pad after pad. And cramps, don't you even care, Kenny?"

"Her menstrual periods!" KGB was spitting now. He tore his gloves off and tossed them on the ground. "Good God, now stop. I am getting so flustrated."

The anesthesiologist continued ventilating the patient. Nurses continued to circulate. Lee W. asked for the equipment to perform the so-called Hickok maneuver. There was a hush in the room. Everyone was embarrassed. No one said a thing.

"Those menstrual periods are basic to her nature. Kenny, you never understood your own daughter. That broke us up. Gwendolen's face is breaking out again. Zits all over her face. She isn't eating, Kenny."

"Good. Gwendolen is a cow, Louise. Maybe not eating is a good thing. You always plunk issues with me. Y'all, she lives with you. And we split 'cause you screwed Harold Terry."

"You left me, if you recall, Kenny. For that whore from Argentina."

KGB was livid and hyperventilating under his mask. He stomped his little feet, tearing off his shoe covers. The chairman ripped the gown off, throwing it on the floor. He then grabbed the phone from the receiver. "Never call here again, bitch!"

The chairman stomped into the hallway and scrubbed again. When he returned, he was calmer. His face was a dull tomato color. Fogged glasses hung on his face. As the scrub nurse gowned and gloved him, the phone rang again.

Dr. Forling picked up the phone. "It is Louise again, Ken."

"Don't you hang up on me, you tweezle. Hawaii, she wants to go to Hawaii, Kenny."

"That Hawaii trip is to the American Urologic Association's Western Section meeting. I'm getting the Golden Penis Award, for heavens sake. I will not be attending with Miss Gwendolyn. She'll have to go with the flow. Goodbye" KGB grabbed the phone and pryed it off the wall, dashing it to the floor.

No one spoke as the two surgeons completed the surgery.

•   •   •   •   •

"It will be just a tug, Mr. Huan." Wei was lying on his side. The tube remained clamped for 24 hours. The urinary output in his stoma bag picked up during that period. When they removed the clamp, little residual flowed out of it. Urine was then successfully draining down the ureter and into the ileal conduit. Jackson pulled the nephrostomy tube from Wei's flank.

Wei sat up on the bed. Jackson taped a dry gauze over the nephrostomy tube site. "Thanks, Dr. Cooper. Anything to watch for at home?"

"Fever, that is the big thing. We will send you home with a week's supply of antibiotics. Take your temperature daily. Call me if it is over 100. No straining for a month, Mr. Huan. Drink a lot of fluids. You may have some blood in your bag now and again until you are totally healed inside. I will call you tomorrow to see how you are. We have a clinic appointment for you next week. Get a KUB that morning before your appointment and hand carry it to the clinic."

"Can I see Maurice before I leave?" There was nothing but bad news for Maurice Latinsky. He had a lung infection with pneumonia. His HIV status was declining. He was now in the isolation room. They allowed little traffic into his room.

Jackson grabbed the phone at the bedside and called the nursing station. "Despite wearing a mask, he is still visible in the doorway. Is that right?"

Wei scooted down the hallway with Jackson close behind. Wei was wearing his gift. The German helmet represents Maurice's delusional life. Jackson and Wei placed surgical masks over their faces. Jackson held the door open.

Wei strained to see Maurice in the darkened room. He lay on his bed, apparently asleep. He soon smiled at the two men. "Hi, Wei. Nice hat."

Wei waved to his friend. "I will visit you often."

•　　•　　•　　•　　•

Septra is a combination antibiotic of sulfamethoxazole and Trimethoprim. Also known as Bactrim, it is the drug of choice in pneumocystis pneumonia. The plan was to treat Maurice with intravenous Septra and Prednisone, a cortisone medication, for 21 days. Many HIV/AIDS patients with this pneumonia responded to the regime.

Jackson and Chris put on gowns, masks, and gloves and entered Maurice's room. As was the patient's desire, it was cold inside. The patient was sitting in the bedside recliner. The first IV of Septra was infusing. He was eating his breakfast and reading the Bible.

"Hi, Dr. Cooper. Hi Dr. Chris, how am I doing this morning?"

"You look pretty good." Still wasted, coughing, and perspiring, Chris was encouraging the man.

"How is the book, Maurice?"

"I am Jewish, Dr. Cooper. The beginning, I know. The ending is not so familiar."

Jackson picked up the Bible. It was a New King James leather-bound version. Maurice was reading in Genesis. He turned to John 3:16 and read. "For God so loved the world that he gave His only begotten Son, that whosoever believeth in Him should not perish, but have eternal life."

"Do you believe that, Dr. Cooper?"

"Yes, I do, Maurice. I truly do."

CHAPTER 21

Jackson scanned the ER board for the stone patient he was called about. It listed the name, diagnosis, and ER room currently being treated in the department. There was but one stone patient documented, Theodor Kocher.

Theodor Kocher spurred a memory of last year's general surgery rotation. The Kocher maneuver mobilized the duodenum, allowing surgical access to the pancreas. Jackson even read an article on the maneuver. A Nobel Prize-winning Swiss surgeon named Theodor Kocher published a description of the technique in 1903. Why his tired brain recalled such trivia was the question.

"Mr. Kocher, you have a stone in your left ureter." The man was a middle-aged, tall, blond-haired man with a ponytail and round, frameless glasses. "Are you having pain?"

"Yes. I've been in this emergency room for 18 hours. I have had more Demerol shots, and the pain comes and goes. It mostly hurts. It really, really hurts. I have thrown up several times."

"Have you ever had a stone before, Mr. Kocher?"

"Well, it's doctor. Yes, last year, I passed one on a flight to Hawaii. That was fun. This stone will not pass, I am afraid."

"What kind of doctor are you?"

"I am an MD/PhD in the Internal Medicine/Immunology department. Oh man, it is coming again." The man lay back on the gurney, grimaced, and moaned quietly.

Jackson disappeared into the ER. When he returned, he was carrying a syringe of morphine. "I think morphine works better than Demerol. I will give you two milligrams through your IV."

Within minutes, Theodor felt some relief. "Wow, I can tell the difference. Thanks."

Jackson put Mr. Kocher's IVP x-rays on the room's view box. He was very proud of his new pointer. "You see, you have a three-millimeter stone in the upper left ureter. Can I call you Theodor?"

"Yes, of course. What is that dot up above it? Your name is Jackson, right?"

"Yes, Jackson Cooper. You are very observant, Theodor. The left kidney has an almost identical stone. So, the stone in the ureter causes your pain. However, the kidney stone may drop during your next plane trip."

"With that morphine, you know, I feel better, Jackson. It will come back, I can tell."

"We need to do something about it. I recommend an ureterolithotomy. We will make an incision in the flank." Jackson traced an incision over the man's flank. "We'll take that ureteral stone out. We will try to fish out the stone in the kidney." Jackson further explained the surgery, its risks and complications, and the expected hospital course. He answered all the patient's questions. Theodor was ready to proceed.

"Theodor, what is it you do in immunology?"

Theodor was researching cancer chemotherapy drugs. He had recently transitioned to trials involving potential drugs to treat HIV/AIDS. "There is a drug called azidothymidine we are trying right now. It is a nucleoside reverse transcriptase inhibitor, a so-called NRTI. I think it is promising."

Jackson wondered?

'By the way, are you related to Kocher? "You know, Kocher of the Kocher maneuver?"

"He was my great-great-grandfather in Switzerland. They supposedly named me after him. He died in 1917, though."

Jackson sat in the ER nursing station, writing pre-op orders for Theodor. He picked up the phone and paged Tara Patel. "Tara, how many ureterolithotomies have you done?"

"Oh, I don't have a clue. Well, maybe 30. Why?"

"Because I have a stone in the ER. How about giving the case to a deserving junior resident who has only done three?"

"Well, there is Julie Mc Sweeney, Jackson." Tara chuckled. "Okay. I am doing a radical nephrectomy in a few minutes. Go ahead and do it. Get Lee W. to help."

Theodor's case would not start for an hour. Jackson met Patrice for a quick bite in the cafeteria. Duck soup was delicious, as was the grilled burger he scarfed down. Patrice told him of Buzzy's septic demise. She seemed okay, but Jackson's mind was on the upcoming case, and he didn't comfort her as he should have. "You did open cardiac massage?"

"Cardiac surgery walked me through it." She described the procedure. The ward eventually called her away.

While Jackson waited, he thought about Kocher's research. He walked over to the university medical library with a project in mind.

Helga was his librarian friend. She was blond and friendly. While Jackson could do a literature search, it was much easier to ask her. Besides, she was cute. "Helga, could you help me?"

"Of course, Dr. Cooper. What do you need?"

"See what you can find on this drug, azidothymidine? Here I wrote it down for you. Anything on immunotherapy would be nice."

"Will do. You can pick it up. Say four p.m.."

"Dr. Cooper. The patient is ready in room two."

Lee W. was already in the room when Jackson entered. The Texan busied himself with the man's IVP, snapping the films onto the view box.

"How goes it, y'all?" He pointed to the ureteral stone. "Simple task, Jackson, just for you. We'll make a 12th rib incision, and Mr., what's his name, is home free."

"You know what? It is Kocher, Theodor Kocher. You know, the Kocher maneuver. He is named after the surgeon who described it in 1903 or something. Help me position him, Lee W."

The two surgeons then positioned the patient in the right lateral decubitus position. The man's right side was down, left side up, for the left flank incision. They secured Mr. Kocher to the table with thick strips of adhesive tape.

Speaking to the anesthesiologist. "Raise the kidney rest, Eugene." A table section raised, bending the patient at the waist.

Jackson made an incision. He identified the stone. They opened the ureter and retrieved the at-fault rock. They could not grab the stone in the kidney through the ureteral opening. Jackson talked Lee W. into performing a pyelotomy, an incision in the renal pelvis funneling structure of the kidney. It was now easy to rescue the small stone. Their incisions in the kidney were closed. They left a drain and secured the skin and flank.

Jackson showed Theodor the stones in a medicine cup in the recovery room. He failed to do this on his first stone case. The patient was upset and swore at him. "I wanted to see that F... ING rock," the patient exclaimed in frustration. Jackson would never forget that. The guy called him a stone head.

When Jackson arrived, the literature search lay neatly on the library front desk. Helga busied herself with another client. The resident waved a thank you, and she smiled back in acknowledgment. The search produced a list of ten scientific articles, ranging from the 1960s to the last month. Jackson scanned the document, looking for a good review article. "Bingo," he said under his breath.

Helga finished her consultation. "Helga, could you pull these articles for me?" Jackson turned the list around and pointed to two references.

"Sure, just give me a minute." Helga returned with a xeroxed copy of the articles. She handed them to him. Jackson recalled how attractive the woman was. He was a little surprised. Her ring finger was ringless.

The first reference was from the *European Journal of Immunology*, dated July 1981. Clemmons et al.'s article was: *Azidothymidine's effect on the Immune Response of a Homosexual Male.* The second reference was a review article on azidothymidine by Masters et al. from the *Journal of Immunology* in February 1972. Jackson sat down on an overstuffed leather couch by the window to read.

The first article described a single case report. A 34-year-old homosexual male with a CD4 count of 130 T-Cells per cubic millimeter of blood, severe wasting syndrome, and Toxoplasmosis brain infection underwent a three-month treatment with 300 mg of azidothymidine twice daily. Marked improvement in the CD4 count, resolution of any sign of Toxoplasmosis, and weight gain occurred.

The second article reviewed the drug azidothymidine. It used the abbreviation AZT, which made the material more readable. As noted by Theodor, AZT was an NRTI, a reverse transcriptase inhibitor. The drug inhibits an enzyme necessary for retroviral replication. Jackson recalled HIV was a retrovirus. AZT was an orally effective drug. It had common side effects of headache, nausea, and loss of appetite. Ironically, it could lower red and white blood cell counts.

While just a case report, the first paper reported that azidothymidine raised CD4 counts, improved wasting, and resolved an AIDS-related infection in an immune-deficient male. In addition, AZT was a retroviral inhibitor. Jackson needed to consult with Theodor.

CHAPTER 22

"Where are you now, Jackson?" Patrice was talking on the phone. She was in her apartment readying herself for today's burns symposium at Redwood Creek Burn Center. She was excited. Her chief, James Tyrone, was so generous to let her off for the day. She was a plastic surgery resident and was very interested in burn reconstruction. The symposium would be a reprieve from her usual routine and an educational forum for her.

"Going to the ER." Jackson sounded irritated and exhausted. "Someone sucked up their junk in a shop vac, and I have to sew the idiot up. Going to do it without lidocaine or a pre-med, I swear. Patrice, enjoy your time at the Redwood. I love you."

The ER staff scrawled the name Tommy Tutlinsky and the laceration diagnosis on the ER board. An artistic attempt to portray an erect penis was scribbled by the name. The ER physician briefed Jackson. He needed more information before seeing the patient.

"Krystal, what the heck? Tell me what happened." Jackson stood in the ER office, speaking to Krystal Salem, the ER doctor who had called him.

"Okay, Jackson. Here is the story that I got. You got to understand. They refuse to admit their involvement."

"They? I thought it was just one guy's injury."

"Well, the patient is Tommy Tutlinsky. He's a homosexual. His partner is Tony Terrelli. They are both in the room. Tony won't leave Tommy."

"Wait. Tony is the one injured?"

"No. That would be Tommy. Tony did the dirty work, though. You see, they were hard and fast with the duties all night. I think I detect a PCP user, but I don't know. Anyway, they hadn't had enough. So, you know, those huge shop vacuums you see at a car repair garage or something? Tommy tells Tony to suck him up with it. You know, his stuff. Lubricant was everywhere. At least they had that. He is cut up all over Jackson. I can't identify his anatomy, including his scrotum, penis, or anything else. I think his rectum is okay."

"Oh, my gosh. Please tell me you're kidding. Hey, what about the general surgeons? Don't they want to be involved?"

"Matt Mitchell looked, and he was quickly out of here. Said to call urology. You're it, Jackson."

Jackson moved to the exam room. There were two men inside.

One gentleman was Tommy Tutlinsky, who lay on the exam table. He was about 40 years old, skinny, with balding brown hair and a frightened, pinched face. He seemed to have been wearing mascara; the makeup running down his cheeks soaked with apparent tears. Like an admiral, he wore a royal blue terrycloth bathrobe with a gold logo on the breast.

To Tommy's right was Tony Terrelli. He was quite an obese fellow, with a head of unruly black hair and a black Fu Manchu mustache and beard. Tony started laughing nervously when Jackson entered.

"Hello. I am Dr. Cooper from urology." Jackson looked at the two. He decided against shaking their hands. He moved and stood next to Tommy. "Now you are Tommy, right?"

Tommy cried quietly. "Yes, that is Tony."

"Okay, can you tell me what happened?"

"Doctor, I would rather not. That nurse, Krystal, was very intrusive. She can fill you in."

"You mean Dr. Salem?" There was silence. Both men just shook their heads. "I've had enough of the story. Are you hurting?"

"Like a bitch in heat, doctor. I mean, I guess you have to see, don't you?"

"Ya. Can you just pull open your robe?"

Slowly, while crying, Tommy separated the leaves of his housecoat. Jackson tried to hide his surprise. Before him, there was a macerated mess of blood and tissue, similar to a bloody sloppy joe. There was blood caked inside the robe. Swats of pubic hair were pulled out and tossed to lie on his lower abdomen. The scrotum hung lifeless between his legs, a bloody mess. Something, a testicle, perhaps, was swinging freely over the sack. Blood flowed from his urethra, and his penis was cut. The debris of the scrotum propped it up, like a lighthouse fashioned from a chilidog.

"Well, you are certainly... well. You will be fine, for sure." He decided against examining Tommy until prepped with iodine soap, premedicated, and numbed up.

"Look. I'll go to the nurses for supplies. They will ask you to sign a consent for the repair of genital lacerations by Dr. Hickok and associates. He is my boss."

Jackson looked at Tony. "Sir, could I ask you to leave for now? We have quite a job."

"I am not going anywhere." Tony stood up. His frame was massive and quite intimidating.

Jackson caved. What is the point? "Okay, Tony. Sit back down." He turned to Tommy. "I will be back with the supplies."

Tommy just said, "morphine."

"Martha. You got your clipboard? Write this down. Get a suture tray, a giant syringe, and a 22-gauge needle... "

"Lee W. You in the house?"

"No, Sadie and I are at the beach. What's up?" He seemed to be driving.

"Okay, I got a guy who injured himself with a shop vac during the sex act with his boyfriend. The scrotum is a hamburger. One testicle is exposed. I think the penis is lacerated, maybe into his urethra. Now, I think I can repair this under local in the ER. I don't know, though. Are you close enough to reach the OR in case I need you?"

"You are breaking up, Jackson. Do whatever. I am in Santa Cruz."

"What? Are you on a car phone?"

"Just got one, Jackson. Motorola. Bye, y'all."

"Did you get your shot, Tommy?" Jackson was back in the room with supplies. The nurse gave the patient ten milligrams of morphine IM.

"Ya. I don't feel anything yet, doctor."

"I will dump a bucket of soap onto your privates to clean you. I'll numb you. Stay still while I do that. You then will be dead down there. Oh, well, just temporarily."

Jackson took a large squeeze bottle of Betadine and doused the groin and scrotal areas like a firehose. Tommy squealed as he did. When Jackson began infiltrating the areas with the needle, he started screaming and kicking his legs. Jackson stopped. "Wait. You can't do that. I am going to tear you apart with this needle if you do. Now promise. You won't move. You can scream, Tommy, but don't move."

Jackson could then examine the man. He started pulling parts together with sutures. He repositioned the testicle in the scrotum. The skin was closed over it. Though the penis was deeply lacerated and macerated, the urethra was intact. "That is good, Tommy. You won't have to wear a catheter."

In the nursing station, Jackson sat with a plop. Krystal Salem came and sat next to him. "That was quite an effort, Jackson. I could hear him out here."

Jackson looked at Krystal. He was exhausted and drained. "That was awful. What is wrong with people, Krystal? What twisted behavior."

•   •   •   •   •

The shower refreshed him, but as Jackson lay in the call room, he doubted his ability to continue. At times on his long journey, he felt so defeated; this was just one of those days. Jackson remembered dying in this same call room last year with a syringe in his arm. Thinking he might find his prior drugs, he checked under the mattress. Was there anything else in store for him today? Jackson pushed the destructive thoughts from his mind.

The rhythmic pounding from next door was too much. The two neurosurgery interns, Matt and Magda, were forgetting their pains again by thrusting like two frantic rabbits. He noticed the library reference list compiled for him by Helga in his coat pocket. He wondered what she would be like in a call room.

The thought quickly overcame him. He was calling the library before he could dissuade himself. "Hello, university library. Can you hold?"

As he waited on hold, he began to have cold feet. When they answered, it was too late. "Have you been helped?"

"This is Dr. Cooper. Is Helga there?"

"Hold on."

In an instant, she was on the phone, as though expecting Jackson. "Hello, this is Helga. How can I help you, Dr. Cooper?"

"Hi, Helga. Thanks for that literature search."

"Oh, you are very welcome. I hope it was helpful."

"Well, Helga, I thought we might grab coffee sometime."

There was a brief, uncomfortable silence. "That would be nice, Dr. Cooper. I am off right now."

Jackson was nervous. He did not plan this out. "Could you call me Jackson?"

"Okay, Jackson."

"The cafeteria. Maybe we could meet there. I mean, they have awful coffee. Maybe you would like something else?"

"No, coffee would be fine, Jackson."

She was standing in front of the Duck Soup sign at the entry to the cafeteria when Jackson arrived. She was even prettier than he remembered.

Helga must be Swedish. He thought she had a slight accent. She had long blond hair woven into a tight ponytail, with bright blue eyes. She wore a royal blue blouse and jeans.

"Let's sit by the window. It is quiet." Jackson sat across the cafeteria, behind the wooden divider. He hoped she did not notice. For some reason, he felt he had to hide. "What do you want in your coffee?"

"Just cream, Jackson."

"I got you a bagel, Helga." Jackson sat at the table and smiled at the woman. He was nervous, like a teenager again. "Are you Swedish?"

"Yes, very. Stockholm. A very long time ago. Where are you from? You have a slight accent."

"Boston."

Helga was born in Sweden and moved here as a child. She had a master's degree in library science from the university. She was nice, but Jackson felt so uncomfortable.

When Patrice entered the cafeteria, she hurried to the food line, away from the divider. It was only two p.m. Why was she here? Jackson was very uncomfortable. Patrice exuded self-assurance in her every move. She might think it perfectly harmless. Jackson knew it was a betrayal. He reached into the pocket of his coat for his pager. He switched it off and then on. It went off like a page.

Jackson looked at his pager, pretending that he was paged. "That is the OR, Helga. I have a case this afternoon. It's been real nice." The two stood. Jackson briefly shook the woman's hand before they both exited the cafeteria.

In the call room, Jackson paged Patrice. As he waited, he nervously thought about Helga and his behavior. Patrice was the girl for him. She was full of faith and love. When she was gone from the hospital, he had to stray. He felt so guilty.

"Hello. Patrice. Why are you back so soon?"

"How did you know? Anyway, you won't believe it. A bomb threat. You know, like the Unabomber."

CHAPTER 23

The stale coffee in the ancient urn bubbled and smelled of burnt grounds. A few hard, glazed donuts lay stacked on a tray. Jackson gambled on a cup and a donut.

James Marks was not eating. "You can't eat those, Jackson. They will haunt your dreams if you have a chance for a dream. I haven't had enough sleep to cruise into REM for weeks."

Hospital grand rounds were beginning early Wednesday morning. The subject was something about thyroid crisis' in Hashimoto's Thyroiditis. Jackson was here for the food. The table before him was a big disappointment. James Marks was his friend from Boston. He never ate hospital food.

"Jackson. You remember a guy named Wei Huan? The guy with the hemicorpectomy."

"Of course, James. I know him really well. We just discharged him. What is the matter with him now?"

James reported the night-time admission of Wei Huan to the internal medicine service. "He had a PE. Strange. Wei has no legs or pelvis. The guy must have a deep vein thrombosis (DVT) somewhere."

Pulmonary Embolisms, or PE, are blood clots that flow and lodge in the lungs. Classically, they form a DVT in the deep veins of the legs and pelvis, breaking loose and traveling to the lungs. Mr. Huan's anatomy was missing those structures.

"Probably formed in the lower Vena Cava, James. Look for it on ultrasound."

Jackson proposed the DVT began in the lower Vena Cava, broke loose, and then traveled to the lungs.

"We'll see him on rounds. What floor? You really interested in Hashimoto's, James?"

"Not me. I am leaving this conference. Your patient is on west two B (W2B.)"

•   •   •   •   •

"We forgot to take out his stent." The urology team comprising Tara Patel, Jackson Cooper, Chris Draper, the intern, and two new medical students stood in radiology and viewed Wei Huan's last set of nephrotomograms.

Chris pointed to a narrow opaque tube overlying the left kidney and ileal conduit. It was a stent designed to route urine.

"I left the stent in on purpose. We discussed this before you came on the service, Chris."

Tara was pointing to the stent. She, too, carried a pocket pointer.

"How do we get it out, Tara?" The upper end was inside the kidney, the lower end hidden inside the man's stoma and ileal conduit.

"Jackson will come to the rescue. Jackson, take Mr. Huan to Crabb's clinic some morning when he is stable. He is probably anti-coagulated because of his PE. So okay this with internal medicine. Use either the flexible or rigid cystoscope, grab onto the end, and pull that puppy out. Cover him with a shot of Gentamycin." Tara wanted Jackson to retrieve the stent by placing a scope into the man's stoma and ileal conduit. She reminded him to cover the procedure with antibiotics.

Rounds finished up by swinging by W2B and Mr. Huan. The group entered his semi-private room. Both the patients were asleep, the room dark and a little hot. "Mr. Huan." Chris gently woke the patient.

Wei opened his eyes and stretched. He looked at the familiar group and smiled. "Dr. Patel. Dr. Cooper. I am back," he said sadly.

Tara reviewed Wei's recent course. He awoke on Tuesday morning with stabbing chest pain and shortness of breath. Wei thought of a heart attack and called 911. However, they found he had a PE. His treatment now is anticoagulation with intravenous heparin and oral coumadin. He was breathing well now, with no more chest pain.

"Probably Friday, in Dr. Crabb's clinic, Jackson will put a scope in your stoma and retrieve the stent still in you. I think that would be okay with your doctors, Wei. You look good, though."

There was a lingering question on Wei's mind. "Is Maury all right?"

Tara delayed visiting Maurice until rounds were over because of the need for isolation. "We haven't seen him yet this morning, Wei. But he has severe pneumonia. We just started him on IV antibiotics. I will tell him you asked of him."

•　　　•　　　•　　　•　　　•

The intravenous Septra and Prednisone were on their second day of therapy. Tara dismissed most of the group, wore a gown, gloves, and a mask, and entered the room with Jackson.

The room was cold and dark. Maurice lay on the bed, sleeping. He was restless and kicked the sheets onto the floor in a pile. The bedside clipboard registered fevers of 101 to 102 degrees continually. His blood pressure and pulse were stable. However, his respiratory rate was rapid. Tara noted an order in the chart for two liters of oxygen through a nasal cannula. Chris ordered it while on call, along with the appropriate blood gas. The blood gas showed low blood oxygen. It did not surprise her.

Maurice began coughing violently. He struggled, but sat up. After his head cleared, he smiled. "Dr. Patel. Dr. Cooper. Welcome. I was dreaming again. The usual, but this time my motorbike wouldn't start. The Goons caught me."

Maurice appeared worse than when last seen. His weight was down another two pounds. His hair fell out even more. Perhaps a clean shave of his head was the answer. His gums were red and friable. The lesion on his nose was growing and looked likely to bleed.

Maurice coughed in a violent paroxysm, laboring for a breath as he did. Finally, a green, blood-tinged wad of sputum appeared. "Do you think the antibiotic is helping?" Maurice looked hopeful as he spit the package of sputum into a tissue.

"It is too early, Maurice." Jackson read about the use of Septra in pneumocystis pneumonia. "You can expect actually to get a little worse, Maurice. Just a few days, maybe a week. Then they say 80% get better."

Tara and Jackson removed their gowns, gloves, and masks in the hallway. A big red contamination trash can stood by the door for that purpose.

Chris was waiting for the two physicians. Last night, I adjusted his intake to two liters. His blood gas pO2 was only 53 on room air. I will repeat the gas on the nasal cannula and adjust the O2 accordingly."

"Good plan. Do we have a recent CD4?"

"Pretty much stable. It was 58 last night."

"Get Derm to biopsy that lesion on his nose, Chris. It's probably a Kaposi's sarcoma. I'm unsure how to handle it, though. Is that stuff about getting worse at the beginning of therapy and the 80% rate correct, Jackson?"

"That's what I read in the infectious disease note. Maurice has definitely progressed since I saw him on Monday."

•   •   •   •   •

Patrice infused two milligrams of morphine through Cam's IV as a premed. She then unwrapped his gauze-covered face for the first time since his STSG. Underneath were large swatches of yellow petroleum-coated Xeroform gauze. She gently removed these with sterile forceps.

What she observed was mostly encouraging. Grafts were intact, adherent to underlying tissue, progressing well. She gazed at the man's sole eye. He was hopeful appearing, and he encouragingly shook his head.

"Your skin grafts look good, Cam. Pretty much the whole area is on the way to taking. I am going to redress the wound. Do you have any questions?"

Cam nodded his head yes. Patrice put her clipboard with paper in his hand. She took a pen from her coat pocket.

Cam wrote just one sentence. Thanks, Dr. Summers.

As Patrice was leaving, she looked at Cam's catheter. It was a suprapubic tube entering the bladder. It was functioning well, but she wanted to eliminate as many tubes as possible. She recalled the trouble that she and Jackson had passing a Foley. There was an obstruction, a stricture, in the urethra.

She looked at Cam and asked: "Did you have trouble peeing at home, Cam?"

Cam looked at her. Through the bulky dressing, she wondered if he might be laughing. He took her clipboard and wrote: *I had the clap a bunch.*

Now she knew. Cam had STDs, probably Gonorrhea, and had an urethral stricture. Jackson would know what to do.

•　　•　　•　　•　　•

Filiform and Followers (F+F) are used to dilate strictures in the male urethra. They consist of tiny spaghetti-like pieces of plastic, the filiform, and progressively larger catheters that screw onto the filiform called a follower.

Jackson asked Patrice to prep Cam. He then laid out the F+Fs. "Here, Patrice. Slide the filiform down the urethra to the stricture. It won't pass, so you leave it and slide another filiform down the urethra. You keep doing that until one filiform slips into the bladder."

"Like this? Oh, that one slipped in. What do I do now?"

"Take this follower and screw it onto the filiform. We will start with the eight French size. Now push that through the stricture. You will feel it dilate it."

"There, now bring it out, and switch to a larger follower. Right?" Patrice took the follower and screwed it onto the filiform. Then she moved them into the bladder.

"Yes. We will progressively dilate it up to 22 French. Then we will pass this 18 French Foley easily."

Patrice noted the suprapubic tube as the two physicians were leaving the room. It was functional, but could they remove it?

"Yes. Let's take that SP out, Patrice. Then leave the Foley until tomorrow. You can remove it in the a.m. He should pee like a racehorse after that."

CHAPTER 24

"I will need the 22 French cystoscope and the flexible grasping forceps. Also, better have a flexible cystoscope available. Take Wei's stoma bag off and prep the stoma and surrounding skin. Ah, give him a shot, 80 milligrams of gentamicin. I will be just a minute, Jimmy."

Jackson Cooper was planning to retrieve Mr. Huan's stent. He instructed the nurse on the instruments and the need for an antibiotic injection. Jackson placed today's KUB on the view box. The end of the stent looked accessible from below. He grabbed the x-ray and made his way to the cystoscopy room.

"Mr. Huan, how are you today?"

"Okay, Dr. Cooper. How are you?" Wei was lying on the cystoscopy table. His stoma bag was off, and Jimmy was washing the area. The nurse then placed a drape with a fenestration over the stoma.

"I will put this telescope into the stoma and grab the stent. Mr. Huan, tell me if it is too uncomfortable." Jackson advanced the cystoscope through the stoma. "There is the end of the stent." He advanced the flexible grasping forceps through the scope and grabbed onto the stent. He then pulled the scope and forceps back.

"Crap, it won't budge. Do you have the rigid grasping forceps, Jimmie?" Jackson then tried for some time to grab the stent and advance it out. Each time, the stent would not budge. Using stronger forceps, the stent fractured and left a fragment in the ureter. "Now, what the heck do we do? Jimmie, page Dr. Patel."

Tara met Jackson in the urology library. She put the KUB up on the view box.

Lee W. appeared. "Hi, y'all." He looked at the x-ray with the broken stent. "Oh no. The end of the stent is now up in the ureter."

The KUB revealed a stent in the kidney, with the broken end in the lower ureter.

"Look at the calcifications on the stent. Here, a bunch of stones cover the curlicue end. When I pulled down on the stent, I bet this end wouldn't open up." Jackson again used his trusty pointer to direct attention to the end of the stent in the kidney. It had a curlicue end as usual, but coating it were many small stones. The stent had to unravel to allow it to be pulled out from below. Jackson thought that the calcified stones were not allowing that to happen.

"Amazing." Tara was using her pointer. "Can we use an ureteroscope in the OR to reach the broken end of the stent? It probably wouldn't budge, anyway." Here Tara was concerned that using a longer scope called an ureteroscope would not be successful.

"Maybe with a perc." Lee W. looked at his empty hands like he was missing a similar pointer. He suggested placing a tube in the kidney to extract the stent.

•   •   •   •   •

A culture of overwork dominates the medical profession. It is present in the schooling, training, and the practice of medicine. If you think about it, the individual who pursues a medical career faces an overwhelming task. To enter and finish medical school and post-graduate training, most overwork. This culture of overwork spills over into the practicing physician's life. Similar to evolution, those who succeed seem pre-selected for this behavior. The result, nearly everyone is a workaholic.

Theodor Kocher, MD/Ph.D., was one of those selected individuals. After the ureterolithotomy, a major surgical procedure, he was home in two days. On post-op day number four, he was back in his laboratory and out on the ward practicing medicine.

Jackson called Theodor that morning. He was very surprised to find the professor in his office. The man expected Jackson at 10 a.m.. Coffee and rolls would be served.

"Theodor, what are you doing in your office so soon after your surgery?"

"Well. You know. A guy's got to work."

Jackson took a moment to look around.

The office buzzed with activity , file cabinets lining the wall with a large walnut desk overflowing with papers, journals, and books. The desk had several empty coffee mugs lined up on it. A metal ashtray sat on the desk, full of ashes and half-smoked cigarettes. In the room's corner, there stood a black metal coat rack with one missing foot. It was leaning up against the wall for support while holding a white coat, complete with a rolled-up black stethoscope in the pocket.

Theodor wore a black Rolling Stones T-shirt, jeans, and a hospital-issued bathrobe. "Sit, Jackson." The professor pointed to a chair covered with textbooks. He quickly tried to move them.

"Theodor, no heavy lifting, please. Let me."

As Jackson placed the textbooks on the floor, Theodor removed his bathrobe. He pulled up the edge of his T-shirt, revealing a dressing-covered left flank. "Can I take this off, Jackson?"

"Yes. Here let me." Jackson peeled away the paper tape-covered gauze dressing. Deep to this was a well-healing flank incision still with staples present. Let's remove them on Monday, Theodor. How have you been doing?"

"Oh, I am fine. Do you want some coffee? How about a roll?"

Over coffee and hospital-supplied muffins, the two physicians had a long discussion. After reviewing the clinical details surrounding Theodor's surgery, the professor asked Jackson the real reason for his visit.

"What can you tell me about AZT, Theodor? You mentioned it had promise. Which application were you thinking of?"

Theodor was now in his element. He began a long-winded description of the drug azidothymidine, known recently as AZT. "I am interested in drugs that have immunologic effects. Now, AZT is a very ineffective cancer chemotherapeutic drug. However, it has been my premise that it might be an immune-affective drug. There are many studies. Well, that is not true exactly. Let's say a few in-vitro studies which suggest that it has anti-retroviral properties."

"Didn't someone already prove that?"

"I believe it is. But some disagree."

"Anyone ever used it on a human? You know, say with HIV/AIDS."

Theodor was silent for a few minutes. "Yes, a few case reports, but no survivors, unfortunately."

"What? Every one of these patients died?" The revelation disappointed Jackson.

"Yes. Some of their disease, of course. Some from AZT toxicity."

"What is the toxicity they died of?"

"Bone marrow suppression."

"Neutropenia and anemia. Yes, I read that. Has anyone gotten better?"

Theodor was silent for a moment. "Well, not really. One patient had improvement in his CD4 count, but only briefly. He was the one who died of bone marrow disease. But here is the problem. I believe these individuals were over-treated."

"Over-treated, how?"

"They used massive IV doses, like in cancer treatments. The drug is orally effective. I believe you should take it orally, at a maximum dose of 200 milligrams to 300 milligrams, twice a day."

Jackson got a page. "This is the OR. I got to go, Theodor. Thanks for the information."

•　　•　　•　　•　　•

Wei was concerned. He had a crazy surgery scheduled for the following day. He was aware of the fracture of his stent and the inability to extract it. Tomorrow's surgery, hopefully, would resolve the problem. Something else concerned the man. Reportedly, Maury Latinsky was not doing well.

Wei mounted his board and scooted to W3B in the night. He realized, after visiting Maury's old room, that the man was in an isolation room. Wei agreed to gown up and wear a mask and gloves, but the nurses would not allow it. No one but hospital personnel could see Maury. Wei returned to W2B, defeated.

"Hello, Mr. Huan. I am Lisa, a UMC nursing student. I was wondering if we could talk?"

Lisa Waters stood in Wei's hospital room. She was the nursing student that interviewed Maurice Latinsky in the past. Lisa possessed her blond bob haircut and wore those distinctive red-rimmed round glasses. She chose today to complete her internal medicine rotation by interviewing Wei.

Wei invited the girl to sit by his bedside. She was an excited person, and Wei felt especially privileged to give his history. She was going to record today's discussion using a pink Panasonic cassette recorder.

"Mr. Huan, tell me how you came to having the hemicorpectomy in 1961."

Wei described the events that led him to have that operation. He told her of his penile cancer and the multi-disciplinarian team that performed the surgery. Wei talked about his long medical/surgical history. He finished with the recent staghorn stone surgery and his subsequent PE.

Lisa turned off the recorder. "Now, Mr. Huan, would you like me to leave the recorder with you? You could add to our recording if ideas come up."

At lunch, Wei tried out the recorder. He was soon recording and then playing back everything. Then he realized, why not record a message to Maury? He could inform him of the hospital situation. More importantly, he could encourage the man.

Lisa left a clean cassette for his use. He began his note, recording on that cassette. "Hi, Maury. This is your friend Wei Huan. I am over in W2B, being treated for a blood clot in my lungs." He described his intended surgery tomorrow, the fractured stent, and other hospital-related news.

"Maury, don't lose faith. God wishes you to persevere through tribulations. I understand you are on antibiotics for pneumonia. I will pray for your success. Remember that I am your dear friend. I care deeply about you and your progress. I know we will meet at the Duck Pond soon. Your devoted friend, Wei Huan."

Wei scooted to W3B with his new toy, the Panasonic cassette recorder. He handed the device to Maury's gowned and gloved isolation nurse. "Please have Maury listen to this cassette as soon as possible."

"... I know we will meet at the Duck Pond soon. Your devoted friend, Wei Huan." The recording was a hit with Maury. He soon recorded a return message.

"Wei, thanks so much for the tape. More importantly, thanks for your friendship... With admiration, Maurice Latinsky."

CHAPTER 25

"This is Dr. Lappert, Jackson. He is going to help us gain access to Mr. Huan's left kidney." Patrick Lappert was an interventional radiologist specializing in treating conditions through tubes and long catheters.

"Nice to meet you, Dr. Lappert."

Lappert stood at the x-ray view box. "The plan is to put Wei Huan asleep. Then turn him into the right lateral decubitus position. I will use the Seldinger technique and gain access to the kidney. Then dilate the tract and leave a big nephrostomy tube for you guys."

Using an x-ray, the doctor inserted a needle into the kidney. They advanced a long guide wire through that needle. They advanced progressively larger tubes over the wire. A large nephrostomy tube was the result. The Seldinger technique was successful.

Tara Patel then took over. "We will place the 24 French cystoscope through the tube." Looking now through the scope, Tara commented. "I see the curled-up stent. There are encrustations all over it. With the grasping forceps, I will try to retrieve it. There, I have a piece of the stent in my graspers. I am trying to knock off some encrustations. They are very adherent. Now I pull back, and voila'. Here's the puppy."

Tara placed the stent on the back table. "It is intact. See the curled-up, broken end. Stony junk covers the stent. It looks like it has been under the sea." Jackson irrigated the nephrostomy tube. "Most stones will come out, hopefully."

In the post-anesthesia recovery room, Tara approached Jackson as he was writing a note. "Jackson. That was slick. Lappert was great. Never leave a stent in when you could remove it earlier, I guess. I want that nephrostomy tube to drain overnight. Then start him on Renacidin irrigations again at the usual 20 mm of water pressure. We will irrigate him until his nephrotomograms show no stone fragments. Reach out with medicine on his anticoagulation. Jackson, transfer him to W3B for this. Is there family in the waiting room? "

Li Huan was in the waiting room, alone again. When Jackson and Tara appeared at the door, the diminutive girl stood and moved to join them, sporting a big smile. Today, she dressed in a Navy Blue school uniform dress and covered it with a blue knit sweater. She again wore red flat-heeled shoes. A gold insignia on the lapel indicated she was a student at the Kensington Academy.

"Hi, Li." Jackson reached out and shook her tiny hand. "This is Dr. Patel. She is the chief."

Li shook Tara's hand. "Glad to meet you, Dr. Patel. How is my uncle?"

"He is fine. We retrieved a tube and left another large tube in his kidney."

Li turned and picked up her book. As before, she produced a small flower for Jackson.

"I am sorry, Dr. Patel. I don't have one for you. Please give this Bible to my uncle, Dr. Cooper?"

•　　　•　　　•　　　•　　　•

A sordid site waited for Jackson in the urology library. Julie Mc Sweeney was sitting on the floor with a scowl on her face. She was still in pajamas and covered with a red comforter. She switched her furry cat slippers to red plastic clogs.

Her presence took Jackson aback. He looked at his watch for the date. Ten whole days since her surgery. Julie spoke before Jackson could think.

"Dr. Cooper. These Percocets are worthless. They do nothing." Julie tossed the bottle at Jackson. "If you are not taking care of me, I will fire you. My bladder hurts like holy hell. It is like a boiler down there. Did you leave Wasabi inside? I want a morphine shot. I must return to the hospital."

Jackson recalled Tara's council. Don't let her intimidate him. "No morphine. Definitely no admission, Ms. Mc Sweeney. Get a life, girl." Jackson turned and walked across the hall to the resident's office. He closed the door, pulled the curtain, and flipped the lock.

Sometime later, he opened the door. He checked on Mc Sweeney. She was gone. On the floor was the Percocet bottle. He stashed it in his jacket pocket. Jackson went back to the library. He had some reading to do. A fearful wave of nausea came across him. The man grabbed the bottle. It was nearly full of 50 tablets. Jackson closed the library door. He opened the bottle and sniffed the contents. A wave of old uncomfortable memories overcame him. That feeling hit him again in the pit of his gut. He put one tablet in his hand and caressed it with his fingers. Jackson licked the outer surface lightly. Self-disgust and disappointment overwhelmed the man.

Jackson was quickly across the hall into the men's restroom, thinking. He emptied the tablets into the toilet and flushed. Jackson tossed the empty medicine bottle into the wastebasket. Second thoughts occurred as he retrieved the bottle. He would drop it off at the pharmacy for documentation.

In his mailbox was a letter from membership services. It concerned the patient Julie Mc Sweeney, and so on and so forth. Jackson crushed up the letter and tossed it in the can. He felt it was a good day.

•   •   •   •   •

"Sarah, am I going to die today?" Maurice Latinsky was sitting in the bedside recliner, staring at his hands. Mottled red and purple lesions now covered them. It was the third day of the IV Septra and Prednisone. Maurice didn't think he was any better. A coughing paroxysm began that left him severely short of breath. His oxygen mask was now at four liters' flow. Maurice took a long, deep breath and tried to calm down.

"Mr. Latinsky. No one knows the future, but I don't think today is the day. Derm is going to biopsy that nose lesion. You have so much to do."

There was a quiet knock. Sarah opened the door. Standing outside was a tall girl with a bob haircut and round, red-rimmed glasses. She was gowned, gloved, and wore a mask. "I am Lisa Waters. I'm Mr. Latinsky's nursing student. This is for him." Lisa had a pink Panasonic tape machine. "Can I come in?"

"Just for a minute, honey. Mr. Latinsky has a lot to do today, Lisa."

Lisa handed the tape recorder to Maurice. "Mr. Latinsky, this is for your use. The cassette is from Mr. Huan."

Maurice sat up in the recliner. He took the tape recorder and looked it over. He appeared unfamiliar with the device. "Lisa, could you help me?"

"Mr. Latinsky, this button turns it on. Just push down."

Maurice looked at Lisa with a severe scowl. "It's Maury, remember?"

Lisa looked at Sarah, who was busily straightening the bed. "Okay, Maury." She said quietly as she continued to look at the nurse.

"This button, right Lisa?"

"Yes, just push it down."

"Hi, Maury. It is Wei. I hope you are feeling better today. They say I can't come in. You know, the isolation."

"I will visit Duck Pond this afternoon. I borrowed a Polaroid. I will get some pictures for us. Ducks are so lucky, aren't they, Maury?"

"My niece left me a Bible, and I wanted to read something to you. It is in John 16:33. I think that is in the New Testament, Maury."

"I have told you these things, so that in me you may have peace. In this world you will have trouble. But take heart! I have overcome the world."

"What do you think overcoming the world means? Did Jesus mean there was something better than the world coming? I don't know. When you get out of isolation, let's talk about it."

"I miss you and our talks, Maury."

"Your dear friend, Wei."

Maurice was crying quietly to himself. He pushed the stop button and wiped his heterochromatic eyes. A coughing spell came over him. Sarah and Lisa helped him to his newly made bed. He wondered about his friend. What was going on with him? The Bible verse was lovely, but a little confusing. Wei told him of the promise of a new body in Heaven. Could that be true?

Sleep came over Maury as he laid his tired, ravaged head on the pillow.

•　　　•　　　•　　　•　　　•

Anthony Lorenzo Giordano set up camp in a private room in the corner of the urologic ward, W3B, as he recovered from prostate surgery. He was a VIP that brought his staff to the hospital with him.

Three handpicked outside nurse RNs rotated his care day and night. Nurses extraordinaire was the term used by the often ostentatious but always pretentious chairman of the urology department, Kenneth George Bolton.

The hospital staff prohibited access to Giordano's room, reserving it for those who handled the dirty work, brought trays, cleaned the latrine, and maintained the facility. Those jobs now fell to the nurses extraordinaire and Mr. Ricci.

Dante Ricci was Mr. Giordano's man Friday. He was his familiar, his gofer, and his all-around lackey. He stood just five foot two and was a dark, pudgy man with greased-back black hair and a pencil-thin black mustache. Ricci wore a straight black suit, his coat hanging over the back of a room chair. His shoulder holster and a handgun were visible to all. He had a rollaway assigned to him and was subsiding on hospital food.

The patient's care was off-limits to the UMC house staff. The usual on-call routine did not apply to Mr. Giordano. Routine things, noticed by medical detectives, went unnoticed by KGB. KGB's expertise in urology made it impossible for them to examine any other medical field. So, when the leg swelling began, he did not make the diagnosis.

"Anthony, how are you this fine morning?" KGB was rounding with Candy, the hand chosen RN, in tow.

"My leg is still swelling, Ken. I told you about it each day. Look at it now."

The patient was lying in bed. He threw back the bedsheet to reveal his legs. His right leg was fine. His left looked like an exaggerated Pillsbury Doughboy's lower limb. What began as some calf tenderness on post-op day three (POD#3), lower extremity swelling on POD#4, and POD#5, was now a critical example of an edematous disaster. The entire leg swelled up, from tight piggy toes that felt like they would pop off, to a tense, dilated, dimpled calf that extended onto a massive thigh resembling a California Redwood timber. The skin of the leg was tense, exuding edematous fluid, and left deep pitting valleys when pressed.

"Oh, nurse Candy. I wasn't aware."

"Dr. Bolton, sir. We reported this to you. Oh, doctor. He doesn't look so good!"

Mr. Giordano was now laid out flat. He grabbed his chest, gasped with frantic dyspnea, and called for help. His pursed lips were blue, producing a foamy froth.

"Oh, my gosh. Antony, can you hear me?" KGB began stomping, rushing to the bedside.

Candy raised and cranked the foot of the bed into the Trendelenburg position. "Call a code," she yelled into the hall. She jumped onto the man's chest and began CPR.

KGB raced into the hallway and began yelling. "Help. Help, y'all."

Dante stood, sad and confused. He swung on his coat and backed into the corner, abandoned and lost.

The code team arrived presently. As the group rushed into the room, a diminutive female physician dressed in scrubs took control. She looked at

Giordano's leg with some disgust. She gazed into the patient's wild eyes. After quickly feeling the pulse, she concluded CPR was unnecessary.

"Get off of him, nurse. Okay, I want some oxygen by facemask. Has anyone taken a BP?"

"115 over 90, Dr. Kravitz. His pulse is 88 and strong."

Kravitz looked Giordano again in the face. "You are going to be all right. You had a pulmonary embolism. What's his name?"

"Mr. Giordano."

"You'll be okay, sir."

CHAPTER 26

Jackson was tired and overwhelmed, in his usual persona these days. He was sick about flushing the Percocet, still seeing them disappear down the toilet. The man could benefit from having several tablets. He wished it was Julie Mc Sweeney that he purged into the sewer. Yet, he felt strength in the action, something he couldn't have done weeks ago.

A bulletin board with medical center announcements stood at the entrance to UMC by the cafeteria. Jackson Cooper stared at one event that he thought might change medical history.

Azidothymidine, an Interesting Anti-Retroviral Therapeutic.
Internal Medicine Grand Rounds
Theodor Kocher, MD/PhD
Saturday, November 2, 1983
Harrison Auditorium
8:00 a.m.

Ancient coffee and stale donuts beckoned him. He faced another grueling night on call. Could he talk Tara into early morning rounds, then swing by the auditorium? He would invite Patrice. While early, she might make the presentation.

There were no donuts, just someone's excuse for chocolate chip cookies. He stood at the coffee urn, wondering if the ancient cauldron was creating a potion worthy of his consumption. The wonder of caffeine stimulation won him over.

Few people were attending. The buzz was definitely not present. The seats were empty, but he was early. He chose a seat by the door in case she arrived. She touched him on his shoulder as she collapsed in the seat to his right.

"I can't take that coffee, Jackson. They might think about setting out tea bags next time." Patrice picked up one of Jackson's lonely cookies and took a bite. After a grimace, she set it and the unchewed bite back on his napkin.

Theodor was a little late. He entered the auditorium and hurried down the center aisle. He wore a collared shirt paired with a clip-on blue tie. Stone-washed jeans and Birkenstocks completed his morning attire. The professor struggled with a stack of journals, setting them on the floor. No heavy lifting flashed through Jackson's surgical brain.

"I guess we should start."

Theodor was very quiet. His voice did not project. A man with a toupee hurriedly gave him a microphone.

"Thank you, Malcolm. Well, we have quite a turnout this morning."

Jackson looked over at the audience. A bit of an overstatement, he suspected.

"Today, we are discussing an interesting group of anti-viral therapeutic agents. Is this on?" Theodor tapped the mic to ensure its function. "Okay. Well..." Theodor began by discussing viruses, their structure, and their classification. Retroviruses were a sub-type with disease-producing properties. He talked about the class of drugs known as anti-retroviral agents.

Midway through the presentation, Jackson could sense that he was losing Patrice. The girl was trying to stay awake, but she was nodding off. She also survived an all-nighter. Patrice grabbed and drank some of Jackson's cold coffee.

"That brings us to one of my favorite therapeutics, azidothymidine..."

There was polite applause at the conclusion. The room was clearing out. Patrice stood up and excused herself. She was due on the ward.

"That was interesting, Theodor. I want to discuss something with you. Could we sit for a moment?"

"Sure, Jackson, what's up?"

"An HIV/AIDS patient has been on the urology service for three months. He had a fever and a renal mass, later confirmed as a tuberculous abscess. He had a long post-op course, with continuing fever and recurrent TB abscess formation. But the doctors re-explored him and drained and excised the abscess and infected ureter. He has actually done very well. Until recently. The patient now has pneumocystis pneumonia and is on IV Septra and corticosteroids. He is wasting away. He has several Kaposis and dementia as well."

"Let me stop you. What does his serology look like?"

"Well, not good. His white blood count hoovers in the low rage. His lymphocytes are low, and his CD4 count is right around 60. I didn't know they could go so low."

"I have seen them near zero, but they don't do well. Listen, I can tell where you are going with this. I am looking for an AZT candidate. But someone with some hope for survival. This guy, what's his name?"

"Maurice. Maurice Latinsky. He's on W3B in an isolation room."

"I don't know. He's an unlikely survivor. We need to present him to the Compassionate Use Committee and make a strong case. I'll check him out and let you know."

•   •   •   •   •

The IV Septra and the Prednisone had little effect. His fever was persistent, his cough productive, and his need for supplemental oxygen was progressive. The dermatologist's biopsy of his nasal lesion was consistent with Kaposi's sarcoma (KS).

KS is cancer associated with prior Herpes virus infection and HIV/AIDS. While a tumor and a concern on its own, its real significance lay in predicting the patient's immune status. The presence of KS is a grave sign. Maurice's immune system was sick.

"Please, I must see Maury." Freddie Bishop was frantic. He had not seen his friend in a week. The placement of Maurice in isolation prevented visitors, including his partner. "Can you at least give these to him?" The vase of yellow daffodils would wilt on Maurice's nightstand.

Wei was frantic as well. His daily taped messages to Maurice were coming back without response. Maurice did not return the message. Wei himself made daily improvements. His pulmonary embolism was responding to anticoagulation. Renacidin irrigations were soon to be discontinued. The doctors would soon discharge him. The situation with his friend, however, was ominous.

•   •   •   •   •

The transfer of Anthony Lorenzo Giordano from his private urology room to the internal medicine service was, perhaps, a lifesaving move. While on urology and KGB's personal care, he developed a massive deep vein thrombosis in his left leg. The morning's pulmonary embolism (PE) resulted from a leg vein clot traveling to the lungs. Sudden death was often the result of similar PEs. KGB stumbled into recognition of the event at its onset, and his transfer allowed expert treatment of this possibly lethal surgical complication. Negligence was now this lawyer's accusation.

"This is an insult and a slur that Giordano will quickly regret. Nurse, back away." KGB announced his intention to continue attending the patient. Resistance met him at the patient's door.

While attempting to restrain the strong man, the nurse notified Dr. Bolton that Mr. Giordano had relieved him of his duties.

KGB was stomping and fuming. He spit as he yelled. "I'll have your nursing stripes, you bedpan lackey." He flung his old leather briefcase against the door and entered the room.

Dante Ricci would have nothing of this. He stood inside the door, brandishing his handgun. "Ya had your chance, you careless fool. The boss's leg looks like an overstuffed meatball. He told you every day. You worthless excuse for a doctor. Get out of our sight. He'll see you in court."

KGB backed away. He picked up his briefcase, turned, and waddled away. His dream of substantial donations to the Kenneth George Bolton Urologic Fund was suddenly in question.

•   •   •   •   •

In 1981 there were 270 reported cases of severe immune deficiency among gay men, with 121 individuals dead by the end of the year. Many of these cases occurred in Northern California. Researchers didn't develop a serologic test for HIV until March 1985. The diagnosis of HIV/AIDS in 1983 relied upon the assay of known measures of immune function, such as white blood cell and lymphocyte counts. The presence of AIDS-related diseases such as KS and pneumocystis pneumonia supported the diagnosis.

"Doctor, here is Mr. Latinsky's hospital chart."

"Thanks. Is this his outpatient chart?" Theodor Kocher sat in the nursing station and reviewed Maurice's records. His chart was thick, having been in the hospital for three months. Dr. Kocher agreed with the diagnosis of Acquired Immunodeficiency Syndrome, or AIDS, secondary to Human Immunodeficiency Virus, or HIV.

The patient was in the sole isolation room on the ward. Theodor donned a gown, gloves, and mask and entered through the door. The nurse was busy attending to Maurice's IV. She acknowledged the doctor, who pulled up a chair and sat at the bedside.

"Mr. Latinsky, I am Dr. Kocher from the Department of Immunology. Are you doing all right today?"

Maurice looked at the doctor. He was wearing an oxygen facemask at all times now. Multiple purplish lesions were present on his face and hands. With time, he lost his remaining hair. He had wasted away, now weighing only 78 pounds. Maurice looked at Theodor with some hope, however. His one green and one brown eye cast back with a slight sparkle. "I must admit that I have been better, Doc."

CHAPTER 27

Jackson washed the crud off his trusty red VW Beetle. He changed the oil and tuned the bug up. He placed a bouquet in the front car boot for later. With great care, Jackson arranged a perfect night for two UMC residents.

When he held Patrice's car door open for her, he realized she was a beautiful princess. He hoped she was ready for a night she would never forget.

She wore her hair in a layered manner, with soft open curls. Her choice of eyeliner and mascara beautifully emphasized her green eyes, and sparkling burgundy lipstick finished the picture. She wore a black and white polka-dotted suit with oversized shoulders, accessorized with a thin black belt, a small black clutch bag, and black high-heeled pumps. Finishing her apparel was her short black, silver studded leather jacket.

Jackson that night wore very much his usual. This included a button-down long-sleeved avocado green shirt, brown and green striped narrow tie, and brown corduroy pants. His dark leather coat was ready for some fun. Lee W. had a boot for each day. Jackson was jealous of him. He, therefore, splurged on a new pair of ostrich skin cowboy boots.

It was a beautiful night with vivid stars and a soft, cool breeze. They headed north on Interstate 101, speeding towards their favorite area of Fisherman's Warf. Bistro Boudin outstandingly combined peaceful dark wood accents and clear, full views of the San Francisco Bay. The selection of cuisine was enormous, with fish and American dishes dominating the menu.

They sat in the bar before dinner. It gave a panoramic view of the water and Fisherman's Warf. A blazing fireplace set a rustic tone. "Here is some bread to begin with. What drinks can I bring you?"

"I think I will have an Old Fashioned." Jackson knew little about the Old Fashioned, but it sounded exotic and desirable. He was aware of the orange slice and requested a pair.

"I will have a Sambuca and Baily's." Patrice seriously ordered her drink. She looked at Jackson with a questioning wink. She was starving and made quick use of the sourdough bread. "This restaurant is wonderful, Jackson. Where did you hear of it?"

Jackson was reluctant to answer, but did so anyway. He understood that Lee W. was not her favorite person. They talked before about the Texan. She thought that his influence last year contributed directly to Jackson's addiction. "Well, Sadie and Lee W. came here last weekend. You know, water bottle Sadie?"

The two began laughing. "Ya, what happened to my shoe, Lee W.?" Patrice remembered the departmental barbeque, Lee W.'s date, and her continuous imbibing. She still wasn't sure where the girl's shoe had disappeared to.

"Oh, Lee W., do another half-nelson off the one-meter board. I could watch you dive all day." Jackson was mimicking the girl.

"Where did he get her, Jackson?"

"The pool," he said in a deadpan. "Lotion, put some more on my back, Lee W. Now here on my front." Both laughed vigorously.

"Ew, ah!" The thought grossed Patrice out.

"I have your table now." The waitress placed their drinks on a tray and led them to a beautiful table by a picturesque window. With the fireplace roaring at their back, the waitress distributed menus. "My name is Teresa. I will be right back."

"Look at these prices, Jackson?"

"No biggie. I stole KGB's credit card. He owes you from last year, anyway, Patrice. Remember intubating her on the floor?" Jackson was recanting the experience at the Chinese restaurant during their internships. KGB's wife, Kathryn, was deathly allergic to peanuts. Before they knew it, she was on the floor in respiratory arrest. Patrice had an endotracheal tube in her purse and nasally intubated the woman as KGB stood by in horror. Covered in Dim Sum and egg rolls, the EMTs took her away that night.

"Have you had sufficient time with the wine list? I could recommend a fine Santa Rosa blend for you."

Patrice grabbed the wine list. After being shocked at the prices, she nudged Jackson under the table. She whispered. "What's KGB's credit limit, Jackson?"

"Do you have a house wine? Okay, maybe a bottle of that, Teresa." The wine was delicious, as was their raw oyster appetizer.

Patrice chose a pan roasted Petrale sole as her entrée. The chef served it in a white wine and lemon-butter sauce with garlic mashed potatoes and sauteed spinach.

"I will go with the oven roasted chicken 'frites'." The chef roasted the dish under a brick with natural jus and thin-cut fries. Jackson wondered. "Patrice, why is there a 'frite' under a brick?"

Their meals were delicious. Teresa cleared the table and inquired about dessert. Jackson asked for a moment alone. He reached into the pocket of his leather coat and retrieved a white square box. "I hope this is a desired surprise, Patrice. Patrice, will you marry me?"

A smile came over Patrice's face. "Are you sure, Jackson?"

"Patrice, I love you, girl. I know I am trouble. These last two years have been wonderful. I am sure about this. I hope you will have me?"

"Jackson! Yes, I will marry you. But what's in the box?"

Jackson handed the box to Patrice. "Well, not much. I want you to pick out a proper ring soon, though."

Patrice opened the box. Inside was a thin gold band. A handwritten note simply said: *Soon to be completed.*

The flower bouquet was sitting on Patrice's passenger seat as they left.

•　　•　　•　　•　　•

Theodor Kocher was late for the morning Compassionate Use Protocol Committee meeting. He entered and quickly moved to his seat. He was carrying a stack of handouts that he distributed to the six-person committee.

"Dr. Kocher. Thank you for attending our meeting this morning. With five presentations scheduled, we are pressed for time. We appreciate this handout. Could you tell us the purpose of your appearance before the committee?"

"Well. Thanks first for hearing from me. I guess I should say that I am an immunologist. I am interested in anti-retroviral therapeutic agents. Azidothymidine, or AZT, is a drug that appears to fit into that category. Jerome Horwitz synthesized it in 1964 at the Michigan Cancer Institute. It seemed to have potential cancer therapeutic effects, but failed in all trials. Then, researchers shelved it but later considered it as an anti-retroviral agent. The NCI, or National Cancer Institute, had a screening program to identify drugs to treat viruses and especially the virus HIV, responsible for AIDS."

Theodor picked up his copy of the handout. "Now there have been six or seven individuals with HIV/AIDS that have received AZT on a compassionate use protocol. Unfortunately, to date, they have all perished, most from the progression of their disease. Two died of bone marrow suppression from the drug. The doses used in these patients were equivalent to those used in cancer treatment. They received up to 1000 milligrams intravenously up to twice a day. The drug is effective orally at 200 to 300 milligrams per day. To my knowledge, no one has tried that dose scheme."

"On your handouts is an individual with HIV/AIDS, who I think is a candidate for compassionate use of AZT. See his 1979 picture? This second picture is from yesterday."

Paper rustled, and the group commented. They appreciated the contrasting images.

Theodor went on. "ML is a 38-year-old homosexual male. He lives with his male sexual partner in Pacific Heights. ML is an interior decorator. He has been sick and losing weight for approximately one year. He presented to UMC with a high fever and a mass in his right kidney. It was shown to be secondary to urinary tract tuberculosis. His total and

CD4 lymphocyte counts have consistently shown depression, meeting the criteria for a diagnosis of HIV/AIDS. After the surgical removal of his kidney, he has had a tuberculosis recurrence, multiple Kaposi's sarcomas, and severe pneumocystis pneumonia. He has a quite remarkable history of HIV dementia. At present, he is down to 78 pounds body mass, has a CD4 count of 58, and even though on intravenous Septra and corticosteroids, his pneumonia is progressing, needing supplemental oxygen at all times."

"This man is obviously sick. His death is right around the corner, is it not, Dr. Kocher? What do you want from the committee?"

"I want an opportunity to treat ML with oral low-dose AZT. Despite his poor prognosis, he is a perfect candidate for this. There is nothing left in the treatment bag for ML."

"Thank you for your time, Dr. Kocher."

CHAPTER 28

The form letter was sitting in Theodor's Internal Medicine departmental mailbox.

November 18, 1983.

Dr. Theodor Kocher, MD./PhD.:

The University Medical Center, Compassionate Use Committee, wishes to inform you that after the Federal Drug Administration's authorization, azidothymidine, known as AZT, is approved for onetime, ongoing use in the research participant, **M.L.**

Please obtain the appropriate legal consent of the research participant, **M.L.**

Clinical documentation of treatment details and progress in an ongoing manner is required.

Sincerely,

Manfred Kingston, MD.

UMC Compassionate Use Committee Chairman.

Theodor was ecstatic. He called and spoke to Tara Patel. She recommended he present his treatment plan to the department the following day.

Tara Patel informed those individuals involved in Maurice Latinsky's care of the time and place of the meeting. The KGB Hall was open and filled with urology department physicians and nursing staff.

"Dr. Theodor Kocher of UMC Internal Medicine, Division of Immunology, is here today to discuss the use of an experimental drug on Dr. Bolton's patient, Maurice Latinsky. Theodor, here is the mic."

"Thanks, Tara. Maurice Latinsky is a 34-year-old male known to have HIV/AIDS. He is at present on the urology ward receiving treatment for AIDS-related conditions. I just received this letter from our Compassionate Use Committee allowing the use of AZT in his care." Theodor held the letter up. He then slipped it back into his white coat pocket. "I think that the department involved needs to discuss the situation. Dr. Bolton, could you comment on this?"

KGB sat in his rocking chair in the front row of the auditorium, sipping his hot cup of C. He seemed distracted, probably considering his present legal conundrum. Anthony Lorenzo Giordano's unceremoniously dismissed KGB's urologic care while on morning rounds for all to see. This morning he received legal notice of intent to file suit by the patient's legal counsel. Yesterday, Louise served him with a challenge to Gwendolyn's parental custody. The absence of his North Carolinian mind could be justified.

"Tara, go ahead, proceed." It was one of the unusual times in Bolton's reign's history, where the chairman was essentially without comment.

"Okay, Dr. Bolton. Theodor, could you tell us about this drug, AZT?"

"Yes. Well, I won't bore you with all the details. It has been around since 1964. Classified as a nucleoside reverse transcriptase inhibitor, AZT is thought to be an anti-retroviral drug. We just start it if everyone agrees and see how the guy does. I plan on treating the patient with an oral dose of 300 milligrams twice daily. My resident, Khadija Aryana, sitting in the back, will monitor Latinsky daily."

"Dr. Kocher. I am Mary Middleton. I am the W3B head nurse. The medication, AZT, what effects and side effects should we look for?"

KGB was suddenly aware of the loss of his command post. He handed his cup of C to Chris, the intern. "Yes, Mary is right on. These transaminase inhibitors, you know trans-animators, are they as toxic as one might ascertain?"

There was a slight smile on Theodor's face. "Well, Dr. Bolton. Mary. Thanks for your question. Let me just go through our protocol. Mary, the nurses will give out the AZT every twelve hours. It is just a simple pill taken orally. Dispense the drug with or without food. Now the effect will hopefully be an improvement in his pneumonia. We would think his oxygen saturation, respiratory rate, and coughing might improve. I would hope he would gain some weight. But these are for us to see. Now, side effects. Nausea and headache are possible. The biggie, though, is bone marrow suppression. Dr. Aryana will measure his blood work daily. We'll know about that."

"Ya, that bothers me." KGB returned to his elemental belligerent self. He took his cup of C from Chris and stood. Using the mic, he said: "We can't have patients popping their heads off around my prostate patients. And, as you know, W3B is a beehive of activity and cutting-edge research. I don't want this Abdul, or anyone else, sitting in the nursing station night and day."

"Dr. Aryana won't need to be, Dr. Bolton." Theodor knew it was years since the chairman looked up even a lab value. "The Central Lab's computer terminal will give him the blood results. He will check with Mary once a day about Mr. Latinsky's clinical status. He's going to document all this for us. Aren't you, Khadija?"

"Y'all, I have just one minor question." Lee W. was sitting in the audience, noting all the discussions. "How do we know Maurice gives his consent to this drug? Y'all, I think everyone knows. The guy is pretty well out there. He ain't Steve McQueen, for cripe's sake."

Theodor responded. "I know, and that is a concern. Luckily, he has signed a power of attorney with his longtime partner, Freddie Bishop. I'll go to the ward once I'm done here. I plan on getting informed consent from Mr. Latinsky. I hope to get the same from Mr. Bishop. With these consents, I think we are covered on this."

Someone was having trouble with the rear double doors. Jackson was standing along the wall. He opened the doors, allowing in that someone.

Elmer J. Crabb entered the auditorium. He shuffled his way to the front. Those wingtip brogues of his were still clicking like a cricket.

"Where's the damn mic when you need it? You, Dr. Kenneth George Bolton, made a monumental error in this pansy's management. In your waning wisdom, you left the man's ureter intact during his first surgery. We wouldn't need azidothymidine, AZT, or nucleoside reverse transcriptase inhibitors. We wouldn't need any sham modern-day antibiotic bull. Just exquisite attention to the principles of surgery."

KGB jumped up with authority. He dropped his entire cup of C on the floor as he did. "Principles of surgery! You whimsical farce for a know-it-all. You're a prehistoric disgrace. You still tie off the renal artery with construction rope. Take your emeritus containing behind down that aisle. You're done at UMC, you ancient lackey."

EJC was in his element. A sly smile covered his wrinkled visage. He shuffled away down the aisle, brogues clicking. "I say go for it, Dr. Patel. Let the Pashtun follow the man. Treat the fag with AZT."

•   •   •   •   •

Freddie Bishop was sitting on a chair in the W3B hallway by Maurice's room door. He was crying quietly, wiping and blowing his nose on a pink silk pocket handkerchief. Freddie couldn't dress up for the hospital anymore, now wearing just a plain jogging suit with white Adidas. He was just too sad. It was one week to the day since Freddie saw Maurice in person. He could hear him coughing inside, but hospital policy did not allow him to enter.

Theodor walked up to Freddie. "Mr. Bishop? I am Dr. Kocher from the Immunology Department. Can we talk?"

The ward waiting room stood empty as the two sat to talk. "I love your ponytail, Dr. Kocher."

"Ya, I need a haircut. But I don't know. I've had a tail since my college days. So, can I be frank with you, sir?"

"My Maury is dying, isn't he, doctor?"

The man's openness startled Theodor. Confronting the obvious is a rare quality in waiting rooms nowadays. "Well. Yes, Mr. Bishop. He is dying. I hope we can revive him, however."

"Whatever do you mean, doctor? Is there a medicine for Maury?"

"Maybe. It is called AZT. There is a little evidence that it may have some effect on his disease. It is a long shot, however. But you and Mr. Latinsky would have to agree to its use. There are some risks. Headaches and some nausea are common. It could kill his bone marrow. Then he could make no blood cells."

"No blood cells. Maury needs those blood cells. But you're saying that is only a possibility." Freddie thought deeply. "You know, doctor. I don't believe in God. Do you?"

"I actually do, Freddie. It gives me peace, sometimes."

"I think Maury does. I am glad. Maybe he won't be alone so soon. Doctor, I see it as his last chance. Let's do it."

When Theodor entered the room, Maurice was lying flat in bed. The doctor introduced himself. He then discussed his plan as with Freddie. "Do you want to try AZT, Mr. Latinsky?"

Maurice shook his head yes.

CHAPTER 29

Mary helped Maurice to sit on the bedside. He repositioned his oxygen mask. He was pretty unstable, very shaky, and weak. She handed the man a medicine cup containing a 300-milligram red and yellow azidothymidine capsule. The patient began coughing violently into a tissue.

Mary looked at Maurice's finger. The O2 monitor was in a suitable position and blinking red. She glanced at his O2 saturation. It read 89%. That was after that violent coughing spell.

Maurice swallowed the capsule from the cup. Mary encouraged him to down several swallows of ice water. "Do you want to sit in a chair, Mr. Latinsky?"

Maurice gazed wearily at the head nurse. "Must I, right now, Mary? Could I just lie down?"

"Sitting is good for you, Maurice. Okay, not right now. Later, though. Did the pill go down okay?"

Maurice shook his head yes. The nurse assisted him in lying down. Mary checked the four-liter oxygen flow rate coming from the wall. She repositioned Maurice's finger oxygen sensor for good measure. She wrote a note to herself on her clipboard. A.M. blood pressure 110/49. Pulse 102. Temperature 100.2. Respiratory rate 24. O2 saturation, 89%. Weight 78 pounds. Mary planned to transfer this data to the nursing station chart for Dr. Aryana. She picked up Maurice's urinal and exited the room.

Khadija Aryana, MD, was busy with the hospital chart of Maurice Latinsky. He was a tall, thin, dark-haired man wearing a black cotton Sherwani shirt, black slacks, and Empoli dark leather slide sandals, and a white hospital coat. He sat at the nursing station writing his morning progress note.

Mary Middleton, RN, had removed the isolation garb and handed Maurice's a.m. vital signs to Dr. Aryana. Besides noting them in the progress note, he recorded the values on the vital sign flow chart. "Thank you, Mary. How does our patient look this morning?"

"I think he is the same, doctor. He is weak and coughing. His O2 saturation is not good but stable. It dropped to 89% after some coughing. He hasn't complained about anything new. When might we see progress?"

"Well, this is just day three of his treatment. We don't really know how fast the anti-retroviral effects of AZT occur. Hopefully, it is entering his lymphocytes and killing the virus. Well, at least stopping the viral replication, that is. I agree, Mary. At least he is stable. His blood counts are not normal, but consistent."

•   •   •   •   •

The Transurethral Resection of the Prostate, or TURP, is the mainstay of urologic surgery. Performed through the male urethra without an incision, a TURP treats urinary obstructive voiding symptoms by resecting obstructing prostate tissue. One in every two males over the age of 50 years has obstructive voiding symptoms secondary to prostate enlargement, or benign prostatic hypertrophy, BPH. A TURP is a surgery designed to treat that disease.

Maximillian Stern introduced the resectoscope used to perform a TURP in 1926. It is a tubular instrument with optics and an electrocautery cutting device called a loop. A TURP is performed under spinal or general anesthesia. Approximately 150,000 men undergo TURPs annually in the United States.

In the operating room, the medical team carries out the procedure. After successfully administering anesthesia, the medical team positions the man in a dorsal lithotomy position, with his back laid flat, and both legs raised. The surgeon then introduces the resectoscope into the bladder through the urethra. The surgeon uses an electrocautery loop to slice slivers, or chips, of obstructing prostate tissue, leaving a larger voiding channel. Following that, the surgeon inserts a large catheter to drain urine for one to several days.

TURP training begins during urologic residency. It is an operation that requires tremendous skill. Dictum requires that the resident performs over 100 TURPs during urologic training to assure surgical expertise.

Jackson Cooper was preparing to perform his first TURP.

"I always try to use the big, 26 French resectoscopes on TURP's, Jackson. Cystoscope the patient to check anatomy. Then, male sounds are used to dilate the urethra." Lee W. was today's attending. He was instructing Jackson Cooper, who would perform the TURP.

The surgeon sees three tissue lobes when they look through the scope at the obstructing BPH. There are right and left lateral lobes. The central or median lobe is also present.

Jackson began his TURP. "McCarthy says to begin with the median lobe, taking care to visualize and not damage the orifices." The median lobe is centrally located and originates on the prostate floor. It can bulge and limit the visibility of ureteral orifices. The ureteral orifice is a small opening in the floor of the bladder. Here the kidney's ureter exits. The surgeon should not resect these orifices, as that would disrupt urinary flow from the kidneys.

"That is a good plan, Jackson. Always keep the orifices in your vision." Lee W. was sitting on an OR stool, watching the resident. "After taking down the median lobe, go to each lateral lobe."

The surgery progressed as Lee W. watched. Jackson irrigated the bladder at the end of the procedure through the scope. The irrigation was very bloody. They recovered 22 grams of prostate chips. This amounts to roughly 220 chips.

"Let me look through the resectoscope, Jackson. Wow, there are bleeding vessels at nine o'clock. There is a pumper at 12 o'clock. Let me buzz it. Now, you can thoroughly cauterize the remaining part. But your orifices. You are really close to resecting the right orifice, Jackson. Get me a three-french whistle-tip ureteral catheter. Let's make sure it is still intact."

Jackson got the ureteral catheter, a long, small-diameter plastic tube. He handed the catheter to Lee W.

Through the scope, Lee W. probed the right ureteral orifice. It was intact, and he could slide the tube to the right kidney. "Okay, you're all right, y'all. Stop the bleeding and insert a three-way Foley."

In the surgeon's lounge, Lee W. drew a diagram of the prostate and ureteral orifices on the chalkboard. "Y'all did real fine, Jackson. Remember the three important landmarks. Don't resect the sphincter. It is right here and responsible for urinary control. The bladder neck is the beginning of the prostate. Keep it intact. Most importantly, keep away from those nasty orifices. Pretty good for your number one."

•   •   •   •   •

A new morning, a new week. The message was an old tune.

"Julie Mc Sweeney is in your private clinic." Sandra was Bolton's secretary and a tease. She left the message in Jackson's box. Was it a joke?

The urology clinic was closed. Jackson opened the door with his key and turned on the overhead lights. No one was around. He was about to leave when he noted room three's door, ajar. Inside, a light shone and soft music played. Michael Jackson's *Beat It*, it seemed.

She sat on the exam table without a stitch of clothing. Julie Mc Sweeney glanced at Jackson briefly, which felt like an eternity. She then slowly retrieved her Minnie Mouse blanket and covered up. "Don't you knock, Dr. Cooper?" She fast-forwarded the tape. *Maniac* by Michael Sembello blasted from her cassette tape player.

Jackson turned around and left the room. Over his shoulder, he said: "Put on some clothes, Mc Sweeney!"

She yelled, "Don't you want to examine my bladder, Dr. Cooper?"

After a good five minutes, Jackson knocked forcefully.

"Come in, doctor."

Julie Mc Sweeney had now put on her clothes. Her wild red hair and pancake makeup again made her face look like a red frosted cream cupcake. She had on a red low-cut pullover sweatshirt and a black mid-thigh miniskirt. She was barefooted, her big fat toes decorated with bright red nail polish.

"Don't get started, Mc Sweeney. No Percocet. No morphine. No more Chlorpactin. No more hospital."

Mc Sweeney began crying. "You are so mean. Why are you like that? I intended to let you know I am feeling better."

Jackson left the clinic, shutting the door behind him.

•　　•　　•　　•　　•

Wei Huan would go home soon. Jackson reviewed his most recent nephrotomograms. They were free of stone fragments, finally. Despite night and day Renacidin irrigation, tiny pieces persisted for weeks. Today's tomos were fragment free. Jackson stopped the irrigation and clamped the nephrostomy tube. "Home tomorrow without this tube if you are okay, Mr. Huan."

Wei handed Jackson his latest cassette tape to Maurice. "Give this to him, will you, Dr. Cooper? He hasn't returned one in over two weeks. I doubt he is listening to them."

"I'm going to W3B. I will give it to him."

•　　•　　•　　•　　•

Tara Patel, Theodor Kocher, and Khadija Aryana sat together at the nurse's station. When Jackson arrived, they stopped talking and looked at the resident.

"Jackson, look at this," Theodor said. On Latinsky's O2 saturation flow chart, someone circled a value in red pen. Jackson took the chart and scanned it. Over the last two weeks of AZT therapy, Mr. Latinsky's O2 saturation had hovered around 90%. The circled value was 92%.

O2 saturation measures the percentage of hemoglobin molecules in the bloodstream that have attached oxygen molecules. The number reflects the lung's ability to oxygenate the blood. While in a healthy individual, normal, nears 100%, Mr. Latinsky's lungs were far from normal. A fungus/parasite named pneumocystis infected them.

"Maybe the Septra?" Jackson was playing devil's advocate.

Tara Patel spoke up. "Remember, we stopped that last week, Jackson. He had a skin rash from the sulfa part of the drug. He is just on steroids and AZT."

"It is interesting, but only one value. We will have to follow." Theodor stood up and walked down the hall.

In Maurice's room, Jackson noticed the cassette tape player/recorder. Sitting alongside it were several cassette tapes. "How are Mr. Huan's tapes going? He may go home tomorrow, Maury."

Maurice sat in the bedside recliner. He looked tired and sad. He was still coughing. The nurses reported his weight as just 79 pounds. It was up one pound, but he still appeared wasted. Jackson looked at Maurice's finger. The O2 saturation monitor was in a suitable position and blinking red as it should. The bedside readout was still at 92%.

Jackson inserted the cassette today's tape from Wei. Wei's voice began with: "Hi, Maury."

Maurice whispered. "I haven't been listening lately. I am too worn out, Dr. Cooper."

"Maury, I am praying for you," the tape continued.

"I hope he can leave tomorrow. He deserves a break." Maury started coughing. The O2 saturation dropped to 90%.

Jackson did not report an O2 saturation of 92% to the man. Maybe he should have.

Tara was still in the nursing station when Jackson returned. "Jackson, can we talk?"

"Ya, Tara. What's up now?"

They moved to the nursing lounge. Cybil, the new medical student, was reading a chart. "Can you leave us alone, Cybil? Just for a minute." After she left, Tara sat down with Jackson. "Didn't I tell you not to deal with Julie Mc Sweeney? Membership Services is in a panty knot about the girl. She says you examined her with all of her clothes off, alone. What's the story, Jackson? I know that's not what happened. Right? Is it?"

Jackson's heart raced. He felt nausea in the pit of his stomach again. He remembered feeling that way with Percocet. The man thought he might vomit. He told her about the message from Sandra. When he went to the clinic, she was nude. "I turned immediately around. I told her to dress and left her alone in the room."

"Did you bring a female chaperone with you to her room?"

Jackson knew he needed a chaperone. He got caught with the crazy girl, however. "No. No, I did not, Tara. You want me to apologize to her? I can call Membership Services."

"No, to all that. Always bring a female when entering her room. Do that for every female patient. You can always grab me. I will cover Membership Services for you."

Curiously, no one at UMC ever heard from Julie Mc Sweeney again.

CHAPTER 30

Patrice looked across the cafeteria for her visitor. She glanced at her watch and checked her pager, wondering if she'd missed a message. She stood up from the table and waved when she saw her. A young woman stood at the door, dressed in a white hospital coat, with a neatly styled afro and a radiant smile. She returned the wave and hurried over to the table.

The two friends embraced and looked at each other.

"I love your hair, Liana. You changed it so much. I like it. Natural. I am jealous."

Liana Williams and Patrice Summers pulled their chairs and sat. It had been nearly a year since the two friends had seen each other.

"I got you a cup of coffee, Liana. Here are your creamer and sugars. How was the drive from the Canyon?"

Recently, Liana moved from her nursing appointment at UMC to a Medicare review position at the Canyon or Canyon Valley Medical Center in San Jose.

"Traffic, I am sorry I am late." Liana glanced at her watch. "You look real good, Patrice."

"Ah. My hair. I don't know. Do you think I should cut it?"

"Maybe just a little. And where is that famous streak?"

"It died. No CPR. No post-mortem. Anyway, I am so excited. Jackson asked me to marry him."

Liana grabbed Patrice's hand and gushed over her engagement ring. Another long embrace ensued.

Liana was smiling her smile again. "Your ring caught my attention from the door. Congratulations, Patrice. When is the big day?"

"Well. That will probably be in January. I wanted to discuss something with you, Liana." Patrice grimaced at her pager. She glanced at the number before continuing. "Do you think pastor Rickey would marry us in the church? We have been so lax. I try to get there with Jackson, but we never make it. Always the hospital - an excuse, but still."

"I am sure he would, Patrice. Listen, why don't you come on Sunday? I will introduce you two to the pastor. His wife, Charmaine, is really nice. I know. Let's go to Carmine's after the service. What do you think?"

"That is perfect. I am not on call. Maybe Tara would let Jackson off. I will talk to him."

"Okay, Patrice." There was a silence, as Liana smiled at Patrice, quietly. "Patrice, I am pregnant!"

•　　•　　•　　•　　•

Patrice's page was from the OR front desk.

"OR. Oh, Dr. Summers. Dr. Cooper is in the surgeon's lounge. He said it was important."

Patrice dialed the lounge. Jackson picked up. "Patrice?"

"Jackson, what's up?"

"Patrice, you will not believe it. Latinsky is better. Well, just a little better."

"Really? How do you know, Jackson?"

"Well, his O2 sat is holding at 92. Sometimes it flickers up to 94%. His CD4 count was at its lowest, 78. It was 102 this morning. But the most amazing thing is his chest x-ray. Remember when we looked at his film from November 13th? It was nearly opacified with this ground-glass junk. This morning's film is almost clear. It's remarkable. I am going to show them tomorrow at the urology conference."

"That's great, Jackson. By the way. Are you scheduled for Sunday?"

"I only have to round. Then I am off. Why? What did you have in mind, Patrice?"

"Well, you remember Liana Williams?"

"Oh. Ya. What a smile. Well, is she still smiling?"

"Oh, yes, she was certainly smiling. Turns out she is pregnant. We had coffee today. She will introduce us to pastor Rickey and his wife, Charmaine. We got to make church on Sunday, Jackson. We should ask him to marry us at Faith Baptist Church in January."

•   •   •   •   •

Faith Missionary Baptist Church convened in a whitewashed brick building with a pitched tile roof and a large white wooden cross. It sat back from the street in the heart of East Palo Alto. People of all races and creeds attended, with volunteers directing traffic and attendees.

The congregation met in what was quite a large chamber. Rows of oak wooden pews fanned out to form a nave. These descended and revealed a large, carpeted sanctuary and wooden pulpit. Above the sanctuary was a small choir loft filled with singing and rocking choristers. A friendly greeter helped them find their seats.

Choir members dressed in white gowns and black satin sashes. The congregation was standing as they finished up the last gospel song.

"Excuse me, y'all." Lee W. Hickok was shuffling along the pew. He arrived and sat next to Patrice and Jackson. "Sorry, I'm a bit late. Parking was interesting." He shook Jackson's hand and embraced Patrice.

They spoke of announcements at the pulpit. They held a church barbecue, baptism, communion, and Bible studies.

A distinguished black pastor then moved to the podium. He carried himself with a quiet poise and an expectant countenance. He was young to middle-aged, with short graying hair and a neatly trimmed beard. The pastor dressed exquisitely in a dark burgundy suit, matching shoes, and a bright silver necktie.

"I have good news this bright Sunday morning. It is the news of history. The King is alive. Church, can I get a rousing Amen this morning?"

The audience stirred, and a loud Amen resounded. Patrice, Jackson, and Lee W. were suddenly vocal, responding as well.

"The King is alive. He has risen. He is in the house; He is on His throne. Jesus rose from that lowly grave over 2000 years ago after being beaten and crucified. He was dead. However, the third day revealed a vacant tomb. Isn't that true, church?"

"Amen, Brother Rickey!"

The pastor then quoted Matthew 10:33.

"In the gospel of Matthew, Jesus says:

Whosoever therefore shall confess me before men, he will I confess also before my Father which is in Heaven. But whosoever shall deny me before men, him will I also deny before my Father which is in Heaven."

"Whoa to the deniers. Glorious praise goes to those who confess Jesus Christ as Lord and Savior before others. If you confess before men, Jesus will also confess before his Father, which is in Heaven."

The congregation was on their feet. There was excitement in the pews.

"Do we have any confessors here today? Do we have any brothers or sisters who can bravely stand before us and confess with their lips that Jesus is Lord?"

"Yes, brother. Jesus is Lord. Hallelujah, mighty is the blood of Jesus!"

"Let us pray. Father, on this blessed day, we humbly approach you as sinners in need. We are unworthy of you, Lord. We invite you today to come into our hardened hearts and grant us salvation that we do not understand nor deserve."

As the pastor prayed, the choir sang softly. An organ and strings backed up beautiful gospel voices.

"Will you come now, church? If you confess Jesus before men, He will confess you before the Father in Heaven. You come."

"Pastor Rickey, that was a powerful message. Thank you for seeing us. This is my wonderful fiancé, Patrice Summers. I am Jackson Cooper."

The three shook hands and sat in the pastor's office. A panoramic view of the church's grounds was visible through a picture window. Wooden shelves containing Bibles, devotionals, academic biblical writings, and texts lined the walls. Soft Christian music played overhead.

"I am so happy to meet both of you. Thomas and Liana Williams speak highly of y'all. What can I do for you?"

"Pastor Rickey, Patrice, has accepted my marriage proposal. Would you consider marrying us in this church?"

"I have seen little of you two lately. One needs to feed the heart with the Word and fellowship besides dealing with the world. Now I know the requirements of your chosen profession. Patrice, you are a plastic surgeon. Jackson, I understand that you're an urologist. Know that we can feed your souls at Faith Baptist. A marriage ceremony is one thing, but a commitment to your brothers and sisters is something entirely different."

"Pastor?" Patrice spoke up. "Our worldly lives are in chaos. I think I can speak for us. Day by day, it's a struggle. We want a relationship with your congregation. More importantly, we want a more solid relationship with God. We really appreciate what you have here at Faith Baptist."

Silence filled the room as everyone exchanged glances.

"Well, when is this blessed event, Patrice and Jackson, soon to be the Coopers? Welcome to Faith Missionary Baptist Church."

Carmine's Delicatessen was an old establishment on Bryant Street in the heart of downtown Palo Alto. It served primarily an university crowd, especially on Sunday afternoons after church. Famous for the meatball sandwich, they served delicious pastrami, ham, turkey, and hundreds of other menu items.

"I am Dr. Cooper. We had reservations for eight at one p.m.."

"Dr. Cooper. It might be five minutes. We have your table; we just need to prepare it."

The group took seats or milled around the reception area of the restaurant. The place was, as usual, packed on this Sunday afternoon in December.

"I would like you, Jackson, and Patrice, to meet my charming wife, Charmaine Rickey. Charmaine, this couple is the one I mentioned. As I understand, Jackson Cooper is a physician at UMC, an urologist. His beautiful fiancé is Patrice Summers, who is a physician as well, a plastic surgeon."

A beautiful, distinguished black woman shook the couple's hand. She wore a sleek, asymmetrical bob and a dark burgundy dress that matched the pastor's attire in color and elegance. "So glad to meet you, Patrice, and Jackson. This is my daughter, Alexandra. We call her Alex."

Alex was a younger and slightly taller version of her mother. Her natural Afro framed her face with quiet grace. She dressed in a red sweater with a matching mid-length skirt and flats.

The pastor then stepped forward. "And everyone here knows the Williamses. Thomas and Liana are responsible for bringing these souls to our congregation today." Thomas Williams wore a navy-blue sport jacket over a pair of jeans. Liana dressed in a floral pattern pink and blue dress.

Jackson then introduced his friend and confidant Lee W. "Lee W. Everybody needs to meet you. Everybody, this is Lee W. Hickok. He is an associate professor of urology at UMC and my strongest advocate."

Lee W. stepped forward. He dressed in a red polka-dotted sport shirt with a black Bolo tie, jeans, and his usual boots, black lizard skin. "What a fine group. I am so pleased to make your acquaintance."

"Dr. Cooper, your table is ready."

Everyone sat in the restaurant's corner at a large round table. The waitress gave out plastic-covered menus and served iced water.

Lee W. ensured he sat in the empty seat next to the pastor's daughter. "Well, I sure lucked out. You are Alexandra, right? I am Lee W." Lee W. shook the woman's hand. "I am honored to meet you, Alexandra. Well, your father said you go by Alex. Can I call you that?"

"Of course, Lee W. And your shirt matches my dress nicely. I think we were destined to sit together." Alex pointed to Lee W.'s red polka-dotted shirt and her red skirt.

"I notice that now, y'all. Your style and beauty and my luck. That is a wonderful combination, I think."

"I detect some of the south in your voice. You are not from Texas, are you?"

Lee W.'s favorite topic led to brisk discussion, only interrupted by needing to order.

Charmaine began a light conversation. "Patrice. That is such a beautiful name. I bet you get called Pat, Patty, Patricia. Is that right?"

"You're so right. There's Patsy. Then variations on Patrice, such as Caprice, Charise, Cantese, and even Beatrice. Luckily, I love my name. Charmaine is nice."

"Oh, I don't know. References to Charlemagne are constant in my life. He is rather grim, at least in paintings. Michael, I am sorry, Patrice. Do you want to order?"

The waitress arrived and took orders. Many chose the house's favorite meatball sandwich, while others chose pastrami or other delectable dishes.

"Shall we say grace?" The pastor took over, each guest holding one another's hands. "Father, we thank you so much for Jesus and his sacrifice and gift of eternal salvation. We ask that you bless the joining in matrimony of our brother and sister in Christ, Jackson, and Patrice. Please enter into that relationship so that it will grow in the power of your Holy Son. In Jesus' precious, holy name, amen."

The meal and fellowship continued. Thomas and Liana Williams were expecting their first child, a girl who they were to name Emily. The pastor and Charmaine were going on an Israel trip with church members. Alexandra was to sit for her thesis in microbiology.

Pastor Rickey then began questioning the group. "Jackson, I have heard that Patrice and Lee W. are both from the great state of Texas. How about you?"

"Pastor, I am originally from Philadelphia but went to med school in Boston."

"You don't sound like a Bostonian."

"It is my better breeding." With a deadpan stare, Jackson slowly shook his head and smiled. "I am just kidding. I hide it."

After some laughing, the pastor continued. "Patrice, besides marriage, what is happening in your world?" Everyone at the table stopped and looked at Patrice expectantly, with half-chewed morsels in their mouths.

"That would be in the hospital on call, Pastor. Oh, and then more call." The atmosphere at the table was suddenly light-hearted and upbeat. Laughter erupted as everyone imagined life as a UMC resident.

Charmaine then turned her attention to the wedding. "Have you settled on the wedding party, Patrice?"

"Well, I have some ideas, but nothing firm. Jackson has an announcement, though. I think, anyway." Patrice touched her fiancé on the shoulder.

Jackson felt surprised and somewhat unprepared. He looked across the table at his best friend. "I guess this is a good time. Lee W., will you be my best man?"

Jackson's request caught Lee W. totally off guard. He was chewing the last bite of his meatball sandwich and quickly swallowed. After sipping his water, he said: "Jackson, you are my biggest buddy. I would be honored."

CHAPTER 31

The night when it happened was overcast and foreboding. The congregation broke for the evening as the last Sunday Faith Missionary Baptist Church service concluded. Samuel Starks Senior and his son Sammy Junior were among the faithful exiting the south door, their car parked along Pulgas Avenue. Tonight's pastoral message revived the spiritually concerned Sammy Sr., but he still needed to look for work in the morning. Ten-year-old Sammy Jr. just wanted to play.

Sammy Sr. knew something was wrong when a car squealed around the corner from Bay Road onto Pulgas. It was a gangbanger's dream car, the lowered '64' Chevrolet Impala that screamed by the crowded church grounds. Sammy Sr. instinctively stood before his son, but it did not help. The spray of bullets from the AK-15 tore through the crowd, Sammy Sr.'s abdomen, and his son's young chest. The Chevy disappeared into the night, leaving blood, flesh, and injured people behind.

The emergency system functioned flawlessly that night. Before anyone could die, two Emergency Medical Technician (EMT) vehicles, a firetruck, and a squad of East Palo Alto's best were swarming the area. The Starks were front and center. The extent of their injuries was clear, and the medical team swiftly took them to the crash rooms at UMC.

The initial disaster sign was the overhead staff page to the emergency room. When they heard the call, Patrice finished afternoon rounds, and Jackson was leaving the OR. The two ran and did not walk.

The rush of staff in a hysterical mass into the two adjoining emergency crash rooms was the second sign of a problem. A gunshot wound to the chest involving a pediatric patient struggled in room number one. A similar injury to the abdominal and kidney region involving the first victim's father's fight for life played out in room two. Just recently, on the thoracic surgery service, Patrice raced to room one. Being from urology, Jackson chose door number two.

The room stood packed, the sound of a roaring tornado beginning to develop as Patrice entered her chosen battlefield. A young black boy was lying on the table with his legs in the air. As the first surgeon on the scene, she quickly attended to the patient. Russell, from anesthesia, was at the head, trying to intubate the boy. A bleeding, penetrating blast injury the size of a Big Mac was evident over the right chest.

Patrice listened hopefully for breath sounds over the boy's injured chest with her stethoscope. There was silence in her ears as Russell ventilated the child. "Nothing on the right. Good sounds on the left. What's his pressure, Kimberly?"

"Seventy over palp, doctor. His pulse is thready and weak."

"I need a chest tube tray, stat, people." Patrice moved away from the field. She pulled back her unruly hair, securing it behind her head with a hair tie. She removed her white coat and tossed it into the corner of the room after wrapping her stethoscope around her neck. Patrice then dumped a bottle of Betadine onto the intended field. With a gloved finger, she selected the rib and interspace, made a small incision with a scalpel, and plunged a large Mayo clamp into Sammy Jr.'s chest.

There was an audible relief in the room as an explosive burst of air and blood escaped the boy's injured trunk. They established a large chest tube and placed it to water-seal suction within seconds.

"Give him a breath, Russell. Great sounds on the right. Another breath, Russell. The left sounds great too. What's his pressure now?"

"Ninety over sixty, doctor. Sammy's got a good pulse."

Tiffany Moreau was the thoracic surgery chief resident. She was noticeably absent during the excitement, but arrived fresh from a stint in the operating room. "Patrice, we need to finish this in the OR. He's stable, but there is too much blood in the chest tube. They got a room waiting for him. Get some blood into him. Howard will assist me." She turned to leave but thought better. "Hey, Patrice. Good job in there. That's a pretty big chest tube for a kid, though."

Patrice took a big breath as she removed her hair tie. "You think?"

Room two's scene was grim, if not grimmer. Samuel Starks, Sr. had sustained an extensive blast injury to the left side of his abdomen and flank. They suspected a penetrating gunshot wound to the kidney. Sammy Sr. lay on the emergency room crash table, trying to die. He was now intubated, ventilated, with his legs in the air, in hypovolemic shock from blood loss.

Tara Patel arrived early on. "Jackson, he needs to be explored, and quickly. I want uncross-matched blood running full-on. Have the blood bank keep four units ahead. Lee W. is on his way. I will assist you with this case. Meet me in room four, Jackson."

At the scrub sink, Tara quizzed Jackson on the intended surgery. "What incision, Jackson?"

"Midline, Tara." Jackson couldn't hide his enthusiasm as he described a midline incision from the upper to the lower most parts of the abdomen.

"What, then, is your plan?"

"We'll find a tense hematoma around the kidney. We can't explore it without controlling the vessels first. Like Jack McAninch at UCSF. Dissect up the aorta. Identify the left renal vein. Clamp the left renal artery, then the vein. We can then expose the kidney. Probably need to take it out, however."

Professor Jack McAninch was the chief of urology at San Francisco General Hospital and associated with the University of California at San Francisco. He was a well-known renal trauma expert. Dr. McAninch taught that approaching a bleeding kidney is dangerous. He advocated clamping the feeding artery and vein first, then repairing or removing the renal unit.

Patrice entered the room. She mentioned to the group that Sammy Jr. was stable, and they were closing in the surgery room next door. "Lee W. is scrubbing." On a footstool, she peered over the ether screen.

Jackson was midway through the surgery. He nodded at his fiancé.

Lee W. scrubbed into the case, taking a second assistant's position at the patient's foot. "Hi, y'all. What's up?"

"I got a Silastic tape around the left renal artery and vein. With this control, we can expose the kidney. I am fixing to open Gerota's capsule, Lee W. I need you and Jim to suck like leaches."

Gerota's Capsule is the tough membrane surrounding and containing the bleeding kidney. James Terry, the new medical student, and Lee W. needed to use their suckers with the anticipated active bleeding.

The kidney was not salvageable. The surgeon performed a simple left nephrectomy. Moving the now stable Sammy Sr. to the surgical ICU, the surgeons soon closed the belly. Jackson wrote orders in the nurse's station after dictating an operative note.

Patrice sat next to him. "That could have been a disaster, Jackson. What a case. You did so well. Who's Jack McAninch? Where did you pull that out?"

"Never met the dude, Patrice. How's Sammy Jr.?"

"Good. Stable. In the ICU room next to his dad. The waiting room has a crowd of people. How about us making an appearance?"

The surgical waiting room was full of life. Parishioners jammed the small room. Children ran around the lobby. Jackson and Patrice stood in the doorway. "The Stark family?"

Silence came over the room. A young black female lent a hand to an elderly woman, helping her stand. "Yes, doctors. I am Maude Starks. This is my niece, Laila. How are my Sammys?"

"You start, Patrice. You had room one."

"Ms. Starks, I am Dr. Summers. This is Dr. Cooper. We are from the surgery department. Sammy Jr. is stable. He lost a lot of blood, but I think he will be fine. Now, I believe Dr. Cooper has some good news as well."

"Glad to meet y'all, Ms. Starks, Laila. Sammy Sr. is fine as well. The left kidney required removal. He has a normal right kidney, however, so he should be fine."

"Pastor. Mrs. Rickey, did you hear that? Praise God. They are all right. Do you know these children?" Maude turned, slightly embarrassed at her words. "Well, they are just children to me. But doctors. Surgeons. Do you know them, Pastor?"

Pastors Michael and Charmaine Rickey sat in the corner of the darkened room. They stood and joined the group. The two greeted their new parishioners. "We certainly do. Dr. Cooper. Dr. Summers. Can we all pray?"

•   •   •   •   •

Maurice Latinsky was walking in the hallway. Today, he finally ventured out of his room after nearly two months of isolation. Maurice weighed in at 102 pounds this morning. He was free of most of his cough, with a normalizing O2 saturation. His chest x-ray was clear. The CD4 count was rising. Many of the Kaposi's lesions were melting away.

"Dear. You will fall if you don't use this walker properly." Freddie Bishop walked behind Maurice. "You're leaning to the left, some, Maury. Straighten it up, dear."

"I do that on purpose, Freddie. I'll race you to the flowerpot."

•   •   •   •   •

It was post-operative day number five, and Sammy Jr. was already running in the hallway. Doing that with a chest tube hooked to a Pleura-Vac water seal vacuum unit is difficult. So, the decision based on his progress was to remove that tube before he removed it himself. Today was the day.

"Sammy, you got to lie down. We are going to remove that nasty tube today, bud." Patrice directed the boy to lie down. He needed little help as he jumped into the bed.

"Dr. Patrice, I am scared. Will it hurt?"

"Nah. You're so tough, Sammie. Just a little tug. I need you to help me, though." Patrice took down the dressing. She cut the suture, securing the tube without a word. "I want you to take a deep breath like this, Sammie." Patrice took a deep breath. Then she blew it out completely, holding the expiration for a moment. "Then you need to blow it out really hard. Can you do that?"

The two practiced the maneuver. At the end of his expiration, Patrice tugged out the large plastic tube, covering up the wound with a Vaseline-soaked gauze pad.

"That's it, Sammie. You are He-Man. Here is a Fireball."

Sammie took the candy ball and placed it in his joyful mouth. "By the power of Greyskull!"

CHAPTER 32

The fog rolled in from the bay, covering the peninsula with a gray curtain of cool wetness. Pastor Rickey walked through that fog, opened the church, and sat in his office. One month ago today, on a Sunday evening, evil elements of the East Palo Alto community ripped apart their fellowship. That night, evil elements of the East Palo Alto community injured seventeen souls. Despite the absence of deaths, many still felt pain. The church's role as a haven and beacon of hope was suddenly uncertain.

The intended victim that night in December 1983 was the pastor himself. Community activism and threatening actions to disrupt a criminal section in the community precipitated that despicable act. He was the primary proponent of *A Call-to-Action*, a community action plan to rid East Palo Alto of the vicissitudes of life stemming from the intimidation and terrorization of their community by the Sac Street Mongols. The criminal organization was into every evil entity in the community. When they reached for the children, Pastor's Rickey, Charmaine, Michael, and Liana organized the *A Call-to-Action* plan.

"Officer Kelley. How are you this fine morning?"

Friendly but business-like, the inquiry that morning was necessary. The pastor summoned the church patrollers on January 22, 1984. With safety as the top priority, the marriage of the Coopers was imminent. The couple were now folk heroes at the church. Their actions handled the outcome and rescue of two of the congregation's most vulnerable. The entire UMC community was also there for the church and the seventeen victims. The flock, led by the pastors, would protect their solemn ceremony that day.

"We're expecting an overwhelming presence of police and assets that will discourage the Sac Street Mongols, Officer."

"Yes, Pastor. We agree. We are planning for twenty-nine officers and thirteen vehicles to patrol the streets in and around the sanctuary. You're going to receive Officer Nadal this morning. He is my finest and will coordinate our efforts."

"Try, as much as possible, to keep this undercover. We want a wedding, not a military action today."

Officer Lieutenant James Nadal was a ten-year police veteran. His specialty through the years was in anti-gang actions. He was a tall, thin, black man dressed in a neat dark blue suit with a Windsor knotted dark tie and black Ray-Bans. He entered the church through the south entrance, the same portal used that telling evening by the Starks.

"Our force is already on site, Pastor Rickey. They are undercover. No one will sense their presence. Our force has already eliminated two threats. They found a low-rider Chevy Impala loaded with weapons and illicit paraphernalia. The creeps involved are being picked up as we speak. A suspicious black Suburban was circling the church this morning. It is in our possession as well."

•   •   •   •   •

"I will meet y'all after the ceremony, Alex. Hey, you look beautiful."

Alexandra Rickey was lovely that day. Dressed in a rose-colored dress with a matching clutch purse and heels, she looked the part of an excited attendee with her natural Afro just so. "Lee W, you will look amazing as well."

"Y'all, it's cold in here." Lee W. entered the groom's prep room with his black tuxedo over his shoulder and Adidas gym bag in hand. "I am turning up this heat."

"Not too much, Lee W. I am sweating. I am so nervous." Jackson Cooper shook the best man's hand. He thought better of it and followed with a vigorous embrace. He stood in his boxer shorts, his white tuxedo shirt open to the waist. A partially tied black bowtie hung around his neck. He was shoeless, his black socks held up with sock garters. "Patrice nixed our idea, Lee W. They don't allow my orange iguanas,he said. I got to wear these clunky black rental shoes."

"No way, big buddy." Lee W. pulled a big shoebox from his Adidas gym bag. "Here, Jackson. These will please the bride."

Jackson opened the box with some excitement. Black, new shiny cowboy boots were inside. "Lee W., are they lizard skin? You shouldn't have. But they are perfect. Thanks, my friend."

A boy raced around the room. He was Sammy Jr., now back to health and full of energy.

Jackson stopped the boy and showed the boots to the young ring bearer. "Hey, He-Man, what do you think?"

"Cool, Jackson," was his response as he raced away.

"Hey, Mike. Look what Lee W. got me."

Mike Nelson was standing talking on a wall phone. He was almost finished dressing himself in his black tuxedo, complete with cummerbund. Mike insisted on wearing his pager, and despite being off-call, it was the hospital operator. He nodded approval and continued his conversation.

"Thomas, you are you dressed already?" You're so cool and calm. What book are you reading?" Thomas Williams was, in fact, calm. It was his third wedding this month. "Just re-reading the *Fellowship of the Ring*. Frodo and Sam are in trouble. Those boots are hot, Jackson."

A man peered into the room. "The pastor says five minutes, Dr. Cooper."

"Here, let me zip you up, Patrice. You look so good, honey." Patrice's older sister, Abigail Summers, had flown in from Dallas for the wedding.

She looked the part of maid of honor in her classic blue empire waist gown. She was slightly shorter than her younger sister, but still had that full head of gorgeous brown hair.

"I think this is too tight. I can't believe it. I haven't been able to gain a pound this year. But, Abby, do you think it is too tight?" Patrice was stunning in her white wedding gown. Tight it was, but just right. Her silhouette was perfect. The bright white frock was full-length and strapless, with a short, stylish train.

"YOU LOOK FANTASTIC, Patrice. Sam, come here. Tell Patrice that the gown is perfect."

Samantha Cooper was Jackson's older sister. She arrived from Philadelphia yesterday and felt thrilled to join Patrice's bridesmaids as a member. "Oh, wow. Patrice, Jackson will be so proud."

"You look so sophisticated and lovely, Patrice." Liana Williams was just beginning to show in her blue gown. She was smiling from cheek to cheek, as was her nature.

Liana answered the door after a soft knock. "Li is here, Patrice." Li Huan entered the room. She was the flower girl and looked so cute in her matching blue dress. She ran to Patrice. "Patrice, you are so beautiful. Jackson is lucky. Wei is here. I found him a seat next to the aisle."

There was a second knock. "Five minutes, Patrice."

The sanctuary was buzzing as the guests filed in. As Li reported, Wei Huan was in attendance. He recently foregone his scooter board for his newly purchased lightweight athlete's wheelchair. Li had found him the perfect location, a disabled spot just on the center aisle.

"Dr. Patel, please sit by me."

With her husband in tow, Tara Patel arrived and shuffled along the pew to sit next to Wei. "Wei, you look so good. This is Richard, my husband."

Kenneth George Bolton arrived in a huff. He wore a powder blue tuxedo with a matching hand-tied powder blue bowtie. He was so flustrated. His directions were wrong. The parking was a mess. Kathryn was behind the grumbling man, trying to calm him down. The man was impossible. Her testy smile showed her impatience.

Elmer J. Crabb and wife Eleanor entered the sanctuary. He was irritable and voiced his complaints. She was using a walker now, her big black purse hanging and dragging on the floor.

Gospel music began playing overhead. The sanctuary was quiet as the procession started.

Jackson Cooper was excited. He contemplated his involvement in surgeries. Laparotomies were simple, not as intimidating as a marriage. His parents were gone now, and he wondered whether they would have been proud of him.

"Are you ready, Jackson?" Charmaine Rickey straightened Jackson's tie. She had offered to walk with the urologist down the aisle. She was familiar with all this.

"Thanks, Charmaine." Jackson took the woman's arm and began walking down the aisle. Patrice's mother, June Summers, was walked down to a seat on the bride's side of the sanctuary. The entry of the bridal party followed her.

Lee W. Hickok and Abigail Summers were next, followed by Mike Nelson and Samantha Cooper. The Williamses walked down the aisle. Sammy Jr. even held Li's hand as they walked to the front. The boy made a point of pointing to his father, Sammy Sr., as he passed.

The sanctuary then turned as *Here Comes the Bride* began playing. Her father, Theodore Summers, to the front led Patrice. Jackson met her and took her arm with joy on his face. Something about Jackson caused her to look down at his boots. She expected to find the clunky rental shoes she had insisted on. The boots were great, and she smiled at her husband-to-be.

"Let's all pray." Pastor Rickey asked the sanctuary to bow their heads in prayer.

"Father, we come to you in joyous harmony. You bring us your two servants today, who ask you to join them in holy matrimony."

He finished the Invocation with:

"Therefore, if anyone can show just cause why they may not be lawfully joined together, let them speak now or forever hold their peace."

"Let's now read from the word:"

"This comes from the Apostle Paul in his first letter to the Corinthians, Chapter 13 verses 4 to 7

Love is patient. Love is kind. It does not envy; it does not boast; it is not proud. It is not rude; it is not self-seeking; it is not easily angered; it keeps no record of wrongs. Love does not delight in evil but rejoices with the truth. It always protects, always trusts, always hopes, always perseveres."

"Jackson and Patrice, you have come together this day so that the Lord may seal and strengthen your love in the presence of the church and community of family and friends. So, in the presence of this gathering, I ask you to state your intentions: Have you both come here freely and without reservation to give yourselves to each other in marriage? If so, answer by saying: I have."

"I have," both Jackson and Patrice said.

RING EXCHANGE

"Jackson, please take the ring you have selected for Patrice. As you place it on her finger, repeat after me: With this ring, I thee wed."

Jackson took the ring from Lee W. "I thee wed."

"Patrice, please take the ring you have selected for Jackson. As you place it on his finger, repeat after me: With this ring, I thee wed."

"I thee wed, Pastor."

PRAYER

"May Jesus Christ, Our Lord and Savior, always be at the center of the new lives you are now building together so that you may know the ways of true love and kindness. May the Lord bless you all the days of your lives and fill you with His joy. amen."

PRONOUNCEMENT

"Those whom God has joined together, let no man put asunder. In so much as Jackson and Patrice have consented together in holy wedlock and have witnessed the same before God and this company, having given and pledged their faith, each to the other, and having declared same by the giving and receiving of rings, I pronounce you are husband and wife. I ask you now to seal your promises with each other this day with a kiss."

Jackson took Patrice in his hands. A long kiss then occurred.

"By the authority vested in me by the great state of California, I now pronounce you married!"

How Great Though Art sang overhead. People clapped as the sanctuary rose. The newly married couple left the sanctuary and were surrounded outside by cheers and laughs and the throwing of rice.

The roar of the German BMW sidecar motorcycle stopped the festivities. Honking and deafening noise began as the vehicle slid to a stop outside the church. *Mighty is our God* by J Daniel Smith Integrity Hosanna Music blasted from the cycle's speakers.

Mighty is our God.

Mighty is our King.

Mighty is our Lord.

American Flags were waving on the sidecar. Freddie Bishop, with a German Helmet, was driving. Maurice Latinsky, with a helmet, sat in the sidecar waving. They exited the motorbike, stood on the pavement, and enthusiastically waved and jumped with joy. Suzette jumped out and sat at their side. "You two Doctors Cooper. We love you!"

Patrice and Jackson were so happy. They embraced and kissed again. There was excitement as rice billowed down around them. Another vehicle sped to a sliding stop before them. It was the 1972 green metallic Datsun 240Z. Lee W. and Alexandra got out of the car. Lee W. tossed Jackson the key.

Cans dragged behind the Z Car as the two lovers sped away for their well-deserved honeymoon.

ABOUT THE AUTHOR

William Lynes is a retired Stanford-trained physician, author, advocate, and speaker on physician burnout and suicide. He is the author of nine works of fiction including *A Surgeon's Knot*, a Pencraft Award winning novel of medical suspense and first of the Stories of a Surgeon's Life series. His novels *Winterbourne* and *Sweet Amber* are also medical thrillers. He is a born-again Christian, father of three grown sons, and lives with his wife, Patrice, in Temecula, California. When not writing, he enjoys turning wood on his lathe. You can visit his website at www.lynesonline.com.

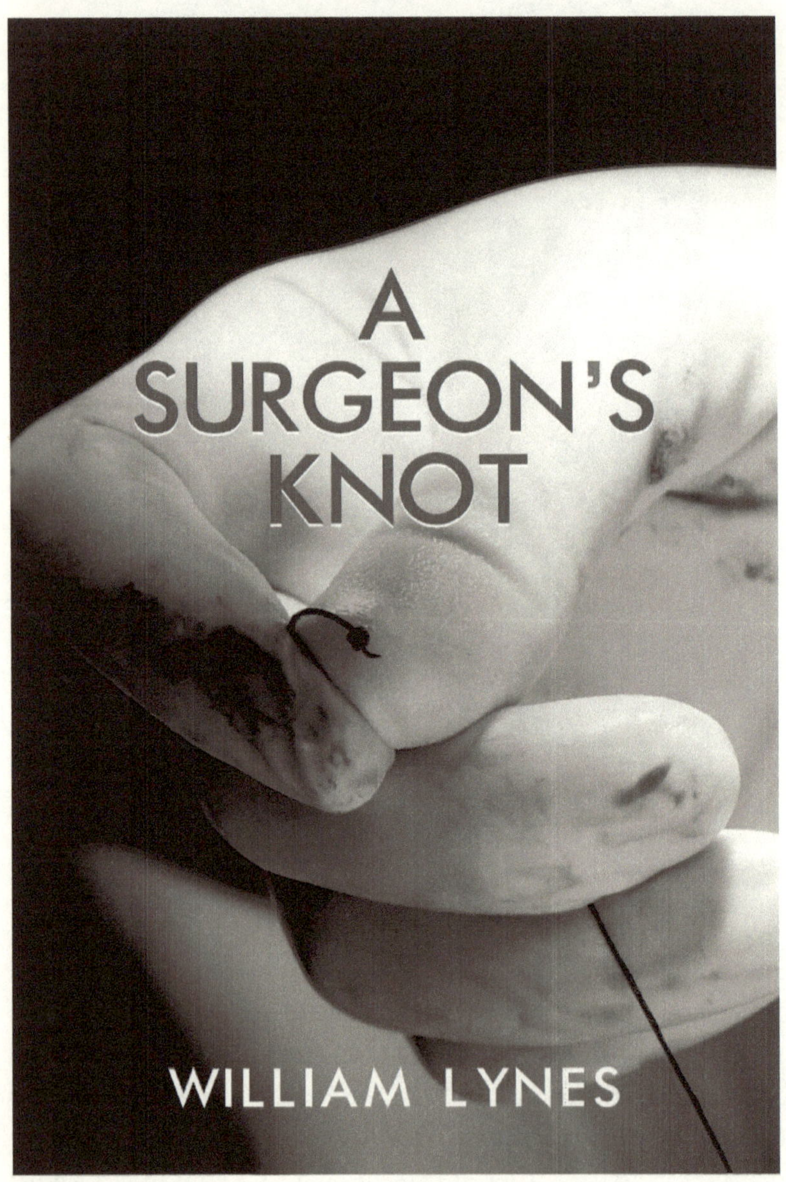
A
SURGEON'S
KNOT
WILLIAM LYNES

NOTE FROM WILLIAM LYNES

Word-of-mouth is crucial for any author to succeed. If you enjoyed *A Surgeon's Tale*, please leave a review online—anywhere you are able. Even if it's just a sentence or two. It would make all the difference and would be very much appreciated.

Thanks!
William Lynes

We hope you enjoyed reading this title from:

www.blackrosewriting.com

Subscribe to our mailing list – *The Rosevine* – and receive **FREE** books, daily deals, and stay current with news about upcoming releases and our hottest authors.
Scan the QR code below to sign up.

Already a subscriber? Please accept a sincere thank you for being a fan of Black Rose Writing authors.

View other Black Rose Writing titles at www.blackrosewriting.com/books and use promo code **PRINT** to receive a **20% discount** when purchasing.